I0695049

How to Schedule a Death

Tabatha Shipley

Tabatha Shipley

eBook 979-8-9880129-0-0
Paperback 979-8-9880129-1-7
Hardcover 979-8-9880129-2-4

Tabatha Shipley Books

Because of the dynamic nature of the Internet, any web addresses or links contained in this book may have changed since publication and may no longer be valid.

For information, email tabatha@tabathashipleybooks.com

Dear Reader,

Perhaps you've heard of me before. Perhaps you've read one (or more) of my available young adult titles. Welcome. I need to warn you that the book you are holding in your hand is not like anything else I have written. This book is dark. This book is intended for an older audience, one who can handle the following content warnings: Implied previous child abuse, death, murder, adultery, suicidal thoughts and planning, implied child sexual assault. **Please proceed with caution.**

Also by Tabatha Shipley

Kingdom of Fraun Novels
Breaking Eselda
Redeeming Jordyn
Training Tutor
Empowering Sawchett
Tin's Tale and other stories of Fraun

Stand Alone Novels
30 Days Without Wings
Projection
A Spark of Magic
Noises from the Other Side

Chapter 1

—◆—

THE FIRST TIME I killed someone, it was an accident.

I was seventeen and driving on my own at night for the first time. The rain was coming down in heavy droplets, the kind that make you crank your windshield wipers up to max and still wish for one more speed. I rolled through a green light, that odd shade of green bouncing off the water droplets on the windshield and illuminating the entire front seat of the car where my knuckles were tight on the wheel.

I saw the blue car making its way to the parking lot entrance, but I assumed they'd stop. I had the right of way—the light was green. They didn't stop. The little blue car made the right turn onto the street. I saw the car. I remember the twisting of my knee as I tried to move my foot to the brake, the pressure in my heel as I slammed down with everything I had.

I remember the snap of the seatbelt, pulling me back against the headrest and holding me in position. I remember the tug in my left arm as I wrenched the wheel. Nothing helped. I slammed into her at practically full speed.

The police officer who was called to the scene tried to reassure the sniveling mess that I had become that it was not my fault. It was a traffic accident. Accidents are called accidents precisely because no one intends for them to happen. He told me I did the right thing by staying on scene. He assured me it was all going to be alright.

I never told that officer I stayed on the scene because the sight of her blood sliding down her face was mesmerizing. I never told anyone that.

I watched this complete stranger take ragged breaths for five minutes after I dialed 911. I watched the last one leave her body in more of a single woosh, something she had no control over.

I knew in that moment that death is the most beautiful thing in this world.

I never expected to like death. It just sort of happened.

Chapter 2

FROM THE OUTSIDE, my house looks like every other house in the area. The garage with room for one car, the large yard, the many porches with seating for two. Inside, you'll find evidence of two people living happily here.

Beside me, the oven beeps to alert me that it has reached temperature as I'm sliding my knife through a yellow onion. I let go of the onion, holding the knife steady above the cutting board. The oven door drops open at the flick of my wrist, allowing me to slip the bread onto the top rack. I have already resumed my hold on the onion and started my next slice as I push the door closed with my hip. I make the last cut and easily spin on my bare heel to toss the top of the onion into the garbage. Then, I open the lid on the potato soup that has been cooking on low heat all day. I drop the fresh onion and a block of cream cheese into the soup, giving it a swirl with the wooden spoon nestled in the spoon rest beside the stove.

I'm just replacing the lid of the pot when I hear the garage door slide open. That is my cue to grab the bottle of Malbec off the counter where it has been aerating and pour two generous glasses.

I smell the wine, closing my eyes to enjoy the expensive cherry and oak. Then I take a sip, savoring that perfect temperature and acidity. I lower the glass and look across the dining room to see my husband crossing the entry into the house. I watch him drop his bag and slip off his shoes before leaving the mud room. He shuts the wooden door behind him, effectively cutting off my view of that room before he crosses the dining room, coming toward me.

I read his body language, looking for clues as to why he's late. His button-up shirt is still buttoned all the way to the top, and his tie is tightly affixed. He didn't hit the gym on the way home. When Henry gets nervous, he tends to rock back in his chair at work, causing the shirt to come untucked in the front—a problem he typically doesn't bother fixing on a stressful day. But his shirt is still tucked into his black work pants that have lost some of their starch as the day went on, so he wasn't working late and stressed about something.

His blue eyes are shining, and he is smiling at me, that same smile that he has used to make my heart flutter since we were eighteen and newly in love. "You got a haircut," I say, proud of myself for noticing the slightly shorter tips.

"I swung by on the way home. I knew you started soup this morning so I didn't think it would mess up our schedule too much."

He's being kind. 'Schedule' makes it sound like we have grander plans than to eat this soup, drink our wine, and watch something on television. He really means he didn't think I would mind. He's right; I don't.

"It didn't." I hand him a full glass of red wine and watch his Adam's apple bob as he takes a generous sip. There's no pause to swirl it or smell it. Henry trusts me to pick something good.

The wine glass pulls away from his lips, and his eyes close. "This is exactly what I was hoping for. I can almost taste that potato soup I smell complimenting the flavor."

"Speaking of soup..." I ladle a large bowl of the white, aromatic stew into one of the bowls that came in a set someone bought us for our wedding over ten years ago.

Henry yanks two soup spoons out of the drawer beside the stove. The soup spoons, I recall, were another wedding gift. It makes me smile to think of how many of the things in this house we have built are a direct line to loving family and our lives together.

He hands me one of the spoons just as I hand off the dark blue ceramic bowl. He drops his spoon into the liquid, taking a taste of the soup. "This is even better than the last time." The words come out as a moan, coaxing a smile from me. "Seriously, how do you do this?"

"It's just ingredients thrown together." I shy away from the praise, turning back toward the counter. I grab my own bowl in my right hand, the spoon balanced on the rim. Then I take my wine glass in my left and maneuver around Henry, heading for the dining room table and my customary chair.

He follows me into the room, drops his dinner in front of his place at the table, and crosses to flip on the overhead light. "How was your day?" he asks. He makes his way back to the table and stretches out his long legs in front of him as he takes his seat.

I smile. "Same shit, different day."

"I hear that. Did that new client pan out?"

"I'm actually still waiting to hear. He is supposed to call tonight." I point to my cell phone, sitting on the charger nearby. "Don't think I'm rude if I answer it."

"Business is business. I get it." He smiles at me again, and I actually feel my heart flutter.

He gets up out of his chair and makes his way over to me. I raise my eyebrows at him, teasing. "What are you doing?" I ask, faking innocence.

"I'm flirting with my wife. How am I doing?" He winks at me.

His newly cut brown hair is neatly slicked back in that way only the hairdressers style it. I reach up and run my fingers through it. Henry's eyes close, and he makes a sound like a purr. "So much shorter," I whisper. "She did a good job."

His eyes pop open. "I'm glad you like it. Thank you for making dinner." He puts his weight on the arms of my chair and leans down close to me. "I love you, Regina."

I lean forward just enough to complete the kiss. One of his hands leaves the arm of the chair and falls on my thigh, rubbing a little through the jeans.

Then the smell of baking bread reaches my nose, reminding me I had put it back in to warm. I pull away from the passionate kiss. "Shit, I completely forgot about the bread. Will you grab it out of the oven for me?" I ask.

The timing is impeccable. Just as Henry stands and walks out of the room my phone starts to vibrate. I cross to the charger, unplugging the cord from the black screen. I shake the phone toward the kitchen, a signal. "I'm going to answer this. I'll be right back."

I quickly slip through the hall and into my office, closing

the door. With my right hand, I reach under my long shirt and into the pocket of my jeans to retrieve the ringing disposable phone. "Hello?" My voice is a whisper.

"Is this—" a man's voice starts.

"When can you meet?" I don't know what the caller was going to call me, but I'd rather not play that game. If they have this number, they know who they're looking for.

"Tonight?" Hesitant, questioning. He knows I'm in charge.

"Done. There's a 24-hour Walgreens right by where the 126 meets the 140. Drive behind the building. Directly across from the dumpster, there's a street light with a broken bulb. Park below it. Be there between 50 and 65 minutes from now. Keep your doors unlocked. Bring cash. Don't call this number again."

"Wait, how much—"

I hang up the phone. I don't know if he will be there. I honestly don't particularly care. At this point, I've invested nothing into this interaction. I take a breath and find my other personality again. I drop the burner phone back into my pocket and affix a smile to my face. Then I fling open the door and slide down the hallway back into the dining room. "Sorry about that. Work. It turns out we do have a deal. I need to head out and meet with the client. I'd like to get this contract signed tonight. Are you okay with that?"

Henry looks up from his place setting, which now includes a fat slice of warm bread glistening with butter. "I suppose I can head to the gym and work off this extra large bowl of soup." He smiles. "I won't even complain about it much."

"You are the perfect husband, do you know that?" I ask.

"I've heard you say it a time or two."

I bend down and plant a kiss on his lips, one that passes a lot of heat. I do love this man. I can't forget that when I'm working tonight. I won't let myself forget that.

Chapter 3

— ◆ —

IT WOULD TAKE me forty-five minutes to drive to the meeting location I chose if I were to drive straight there. I don't plan to drive straight there.

There's a reason I chose that spot. I happen to know it is a dead zone between two security cameras. It's also a 24-hour Walgreens, which means no one will notice a car parked there if it isn't parked long. They may notice two cars, but I have that part planned too. There is a reason for everything I do. Everything in its place and all that.

Fifteen minutes from town, I pull my car off the main road and onto a dirt road to the right. Fifty feet later, I turn to the left and progress deeper into the woods. I cannot see the main road from here. More importantly, anyone driving down the main road at this hour of the night cannot see me.

I throw the car in park just as a popular OneRepublic song comes on the radio. I leave the car running and bob my head to the song. I pull the cotton shirt over my head while I sing along to the first verse and drop the shirt in the backseat as the song picks up. I grab a slightly faded black tee shirt and pull it over my head, ignoring the wrinkles. I lean forward and slip my arms into the sleeves of a black jacket, leaving it open.

Then I slip the plain black hair tie off the shifter knob in the center console and pull my long blonde locks into a simple ponytail. I keep the hair tie low to allow me to slip the ponytail through the opening on the black hat I pull onto my head. By the time I throw the car back into gear and point myself toward the main road, the song is coming to an end and I belt out my favorite part.

The rest of the drive is uneventful. I note a few cars on the road, but nothing that stands out. More importantly, I don't notice anything or anyone that may notice me. No one is craning their neck in my direction, no one tailgating my car, no one who seems to cast nervous glances in my direction at red lights. I'm careful not to follow anyone closely enough to raise suspicion; I actively try to be the kind of driver you forget about as opposed to the kind of driver that pisses you off. I'm in control here, as it should be.

It really doesn't matter how many times you meet a new client, something inside you always quakes a little under the pressure of a new meeting. I can't let it get the best of me, though. I am in control today.

I am always in control.

I slow my car as I approach the turn before the Walgreens I mentioned on the phone, but I do not turn my car into the entrance that will lead to the alleyway behind the store. This is another reason I chose this location. There is a house here, just a few spaces down from the location, that is empty. It has been empty for just enough time to be juicy.

Someone bought it, according to records, six months ago. They gutted it and tried flipping it. It is listed on a few real estate sites. Then, when it wasn't moving, the price was lowered. That was about a week ago. This has led to an uptick in interest. Meaning an odd car parked nearby or someone wandering on the property is not exactly noticeable. The people in this neighborhood will assume, when I park my dark SUV in the small alleyway beside the house, that I'm just looking. An inference I play on as I walk around the front, snapping pictures and peeking in windows. I look like any other interested buyer just checking the curb appeal.

Then I walk. I can actually see the sign for the Walgreens from this front yard. I move quickly, aware of how much time has passed since I disconnected the phone call. The client should be parked exactly where I directed him by now, if he can follow directions. I certainly hope he can follow directions because I don't work with people who can't. This business is already dangerous enough, meeting strange people in dark parking lots at night, without wildcards being thrown into the mix.

At the Walgreens parking lot, I keep to the right, by the trees. I walk with a purpose, my head low to hide my face from the spotty security cameras. I turn the corner behind the building and see a dark BMW, possibly green or navy blue. It's an older model, and it's parked directly under the street light, as instructed. A smile tugs at the corner of my lips. In this business, BMW means money. He certainly has my attention now.

Chapter 4

I OPEN THE passenger side door of the dark BMW like I was expecting it to be here, which of course, I was. Mentally, I tick up the bill I'm about to extend when I note the car is clean and polished. Anyone who can afford to keep their car clean like this can afford to pay me more.

The driver, an average man with a slight beer gut, startles a little when I drop into the passenger seat. He opens his mouth, but I lean across the center console and put my finger across his lips. "I do all the talking," I instruct. "You are only allowed to answer with a simple yes or no. Are we clear?" I move my finger away, indicating he may answer.

"Yes." He gulps. Nervous.

Mentally, I add more money to his tab. He'll pay.

I pull the door shut. I'm pleased when I see a plain manilla envelope, standard legal size, sitting on the center console. This man has been referred to me by a previous client, someone who knows my methods, and he's prepared. That is good.

"You are aware of what I do?"

"Yes."

I look him up and down. He is nothing like my Henry. My Henry is almost forty, but he has the physique of a much younger man. He works out almost daily and keeps himself fit. This man, in contrast, disgusts me. He dresses as though trying to convince women he would sweat dollar bills from his fat rolls in his attempt at a power suit. The jacket for the suit is on the bench seat in the back, and the tie looks like it was crumbled with it not long before this meeting. His white shirt has sweat stains, and I can almost visualize the untucked back end of the shirt flapping around if he were to stand up. I cannot stop my lip from curling.

"This is about your wife," I say. I'm hedging my bets. Years of experience and the wedding ring he is nervously spinning around his left hand are my best clues.

"Yes," he confirms.

I nod slowly, giving the air of one considering. In truth, I wouldn't be here if I hadn't already agreed to work with him. "Forty grand," I say.

There is only a small hesitation before "Yes". Damn, I could've asked for more.

Still, I launch into my accepting speech. "Once this is scheduled, it cannot be unscheduled." A glimmer of doubt crosses his eyes. "God himself could not stop this once you set it in motion, so you must be absolutely sure. Are we clear?"

His Adam's apple bobs as he swallows. "Yes."

I nod. He has more guts than I thought, I'll give him that. "You will not contact me again. You will not hear from me again. You will trust that it will be done."

"Okay."

I shoot him a warning glare.

"Um, I mean, yes," he corrects.

"If we're doing this, cash." I hold out my palm, waiting. This is where he will have his final chance to back out. No harm, no foul. He can shake his head or say no, and I'll leave the way I came. He doesn't know my name; it would be as simple as getting a new burner cell phone and moving along. Or, he can produce the agreed upon amount of money from somewhere in this car, and we move on. There are no third options, no trips to the bank, no chance for him to leave this parking lot without making a decision. All that should have been explained to him by whoever told him about my services.

He fishes along the side of his driver's seat and produces four wads of cash, each one carefully wrapped with the bank's $10,000 bands. For a second, I wonder if there is more along the side of that seat. I wonder how much he came with, who referred him, what I charged them. I consider, for just a heartbeat, killing him and finding out. But that would be dishonest and unethical, even if it would also be simple. I do have morals.

I push those thoughts from my head and smile at him. "Pleasure doing business with you."

I grab the manila envelope on the center console, which I already know will contain a photograph and a name. Then, I open the car door and walk away, as purposefully as I walked into this meeting but with my pockets considerably heavier.

I will not open the envelope until I'm back at my own home where I can be sure I'm not under any electronic eyes. Then I'll know exactly what I'm dealing with and who we're

killing. After all, that's what we just agreed to.
　　　　See how easy it is to schedule a death?

Chapter 5

WEDNESDAY MORNING, I find myself seated in front of my home computer, a cup of hot coffee steaming beside me and birds chirping through the open window serving as background noise. Today, I have business to conduct.

I open an incognito web browser—better if Henry doesn't have access to this web history—and click through the usual channels. I'm looking for information about my newest client.

It's true what I told you in the beginning: I never expected to like death. But once I realized that I do like it, I really only had two choices. I could take life selfishly for my own reasons, essentially making me a murderer, or I could take lives for others. This is what military men and snipers do. They take lives for their government. You don't judge them too harshly because they're just following orders. Alas, the military isn't exactly my scene. Too many rules, too many eyes watching. But what about a hired hand? What if I could take the life of someone, only following orders, and only if they were a bad person?

I can almost hear your skepticism now. You're

wondering how I know this is a bad person. I don't even know this mark. I agreed to this deal without ever even opening that envelope. And you're right, I don't know them. Not yet. Hence the research.

My process is simple, really. Someone gets my current burner number from a handler or by word of mouth. No paper trail, ever. I schedule the meet up. I take the cash, the name, and the photo. Then I do the research. That brings me to right now.

My search for Christina Montenegro, the name in my current envelope, leads me to a social media page that is obviously for the woman in the photograph I was given. A few clicks later, I have the name of the whale who ordered the hit. Thomas Montenegro, husband. With a few more clicks and saves to a carefully partitioned section of my hard drive, I've built my file on Thomas.

Wait, you may ask, Thomas? I thought you were focused on Christina. See, that is the best part of this business. I build a profile on the person who orders my services first. Only amateurs are worried exclusively about the mark. If you're in this business, as I am, to only deal with people who deserve it, you have to consider the source of the information.

Take Thomas, for example. He's a low level manager at a local hotel. He's had a few customer complaints for his temper and the way he mishandles situations. He was taken into police custody when he was seventeen, but that record is sealed because he was a juvenile. There were police officers called to his home three times in the last two years for domestic disturbance, but no charges were filed either time. Isn't it amazing what you can learn on the internet?

Digging deeper, I find our friend may be using his hotel

for little trysts with a few ladies. Nothing illegal—they are all likely adults. But maybe it went too far. Maybe Mr. Montenegro needs his wife out of the way. I don't know yet, but I'm starting to be leery of him. Which means I need to dig further.

It's time to start building my profile of the mark, Christina. She appears to be a yoga instructor. It looks like she's never had a complaint or a police file. The only things I see on her police radar are the same domestic violence calls with no charges filed. That confirms that the two parties involved were always her and her husband, one way or the other.

Oh, wait a minute, this is interesting. There's a picture of our little friend, shared on the social media of a friend of a friend of a friend...but it's definitely Christina. She's younger, maybe college aged. She has her arms around the shoulders of a boy, possibly a boyfriend. Here's what's interesting: his profile indicates he currently works at the same gym where Christina teaches yoga. I don't believe in coincidence. A chance encounter with an old flame years later, a job at the same gym, a husband who orders a hit on your life... These are information gold.

I take a sip of the dark roast which has cooled considerably and click around on a few more photos in more places. See, most people don't put their dirty laundry on social media, but that doesn't mean it's not there if you know where to look. I run a search looking for any other images, on any public website in the world, that contain the faces of Christina and our gym rat. Bingo. Three results come up. One is very similar to the one I've already seen, with smiling faces mugging for the camera. One is possibly a work photograph, featuring about fifteen people in total all wearing the same blue polo shirts with the same gym logo.

The third picture is more interesting. They're young and facing the camera, but neither smile looks real. He is sporting an arm sling, and she seems to be leaning away from him, adding physical distance between them.

Thirty minutes later, I've built and saved an entire profile. I check the security setting of the partition, wiping any sign of access from the hard drive, and delete the history. I swig the final, now cold, dregs of the coffee beside me and stretch my arms. My reasons for gathering all of this are pretty selfish. I'm a killer. If something goes wrong and the police show up at my door asking questions, I need to have material on hand to flip that spotlight onto someone else. Sure, I'll go down for the hit. But the police will want the person who ordered it more than they'll want me. I'll serve time but not as much as I would if I had no one pulling my strings. I have to be prepared to play the puppet card. The research helps with that.

It also helps with an important decision I have to make.

I will do this hit. Thomas is an asshole, that much I can tell you. But so is Christina. Here's how I think it went down. I think this woman is actually an abuser—that's why the charges are never filed in the police cases. I believe Thomas called them and then got cold feet when they arrived. But the ex-boyfriend, possibly minus the ex, is what really sealed it for me.

Hospital records show that the sling he was wearing in the third photo I found was for a broken wrist. He claimed it was a direct result of a skateboarding accident. Interesting, then, that I cannot find one single photograph or connection to a skateboard in his past. What I can find is evidence of him talking about a fight with his girlfriend. When I connect those dots, I find she may be a serial abuser of men. A broken wrist here, a few police calls there...a violent woman connecting them.

Once I take that money from a client, I have three choices: complete the hit and essentially disappear, keep the money and blackmail the person who ordered the hit, or complete the hit and then blackmail the person who ordered the hit.

This couple, they get option C.

Big money, big money, big money.

Chapter 6

AFTER A QUICK but hot shower, I warm up lunch on my own stove and drop back into the chair in front of my computer. Two of the best perks for working from home are fast access to a shower and a stove, in my opinion. My husband, who honestly is a lovely man, has absolutely no idea what I do for a living. He understands that I have clients and that I make my fair share of money for the house.

I actually handle paying the bills. Like everything else in my life, this is not an accident. If I pay the bills, I watch the account balances tick up or down. I can easily drop some of my personal cash into the house account to cover something. Henry doesn't need to worry about where it came from, and all the bills are paid.

My accounts, of which I have at least fifteen, all fluctuate between twenty-three and four hundred thousand dollars. There's also at least a hundred thousand dollars in cash stuffed in various places around our three-bedroom house. Basically, there's plenty of money around here to make sure Henry never wants for anything.

I check the clock on the lower right of the computer

screen. Henry will be home in about three hours. Plenty of time. I use a secure email server to send an email to a former client. I attach a picture of two people seated in the front seat of a vehicle that is exactly the same make and model as the car driven by this very rich, very scummy client.

Fun fact: this is not a picture of the client's car. It is certainly not a picture of the two of us in his car during our business deal. You already know me better than that. There were no cameras on that exchange. I have, however, managed to make a rather convincing fake of this event using images of his car online. I used my editing software to input a few carefully placed scratches to really sell it. I cut the image just right to remove the license plate from the picture. I use a free filter to make the image look pixelated and scratchy, like you'd expect from security camera footage. It's dark, like it was that night. It's from the right location, more or less. Unless the client takes the time to undo all the changes I've done, he may buy it. Now I just have to sell it with an angle he can't argue with.

I click into the message box. *Would you like to explain how this image managed to make its way into my email account? I certainly hope you are not trying to blackmail me, Marcus Christopher from Oceanside Drive. That would be a terrible mistake. Meet me at this same location tonight at 8 PM. Bring answers and cash. You know who this is.*

If I were a betting lady, I'd bet the former client shows up. Marcus Christopher is not the type of guy who knows anything about digitally manipulating images, and he won't be willing to let someone else try. I've checked my records. Originally, Marcus paid me twenty-five thousand dollars to kill his boss. He thought he would score the promotion once his boss was out of the picture. To his surprise, his boss' son was promoted instead. Mr. Christopher decided to take matters into his own hands at that point, punching the boss' son in the face. He was subsequently fired from that firm, barely escaping arrest if the stories online are any indication. He now works at another local firm where he actually makes more money than he did before, according to a bit of humble bragging he did on social media.

Following all that, it is likely Mr. Christopher will need to keep his seedy dealings with me secret from his new boss. This is how I know he will be there tonight. I bet he'll even bring me thirty thousand reasons to keep silent. Especially if I keep up the game that I believe he is the person who leaked this particular photo, making him a danger to me.

I clear all the evidence of this email from my computer. Then I spend the next two hours working on my freelance IT security gig. This is my only legitimate source of income. It's easy, worthwhile, and valuable. Basically, high-level firms pay me a lot of money to attempt to break into their online security. If I can get in, they pay me even more money to fix the holes I find. If I can't break in, everyone's happy.

I say "a lot of money," but honestly, I get paid more to kill people. But this is a job I can report on taxes and tell my husband about. As far as he knows, this job is my contribution to the expensive bottles of wine with dinner and the mortgage on this gambrel-style house in a nice neighborhood.

Two hours later, I've managed to make absolutely no progress cracking into the medical files of the transcription company which has already paid me. I push my chair back, purposely leaving all the files open on the computer, and pad my way into the kitchen.

It takes me fifteen minutes to prepare the dish for the oven, as I knew it would. Fifteen minutes of carefully chopping, opening jars, and combining spices. I slip the glass pan full of chicken and vegetables, delicately seasoned, into the preheated oven. Once dinner is in the oven, my kitchen work is basically done.

I know I have a bit of time before Henry is home, so I head across the first floor of the house to the living room and grab a fiction paperback book from where I left it yesterday. Then I settle myself into my favorite chair, the one where I can easily see out the front window of the house, to read a little. I'm careful when I choose books. I pick books that are light and uncomplicated. For one, it projects the right image to anyone who sees me reading. For another, most writers get murderers all wrong. We aren't terrible people, but we're also not out for vengeance. We're just like you, only deadlier.

When the chicken starts to smell like it might be close to being done, I stand up and put the paperback facedown on the hearth of the unlit fireplace. Back in the kitchen, I throw some rice into a pan, cover it with water, and set it on a burner. Then I open a bottle of red wine and leave it uncorked, so it has a chance to breathe.

Knowing my husband is reliable, I check the clock. He will likely stroll through the door in about five minutes. The computer takes fifteen minutes to slip into sleep mode. I pop back into the office, wiggle the mouse, make sure everything for the IT job is still open, and leave the room with the light from the computer screen still emanating behind me.

I'm back in the kitchen, just pouring the wine, when I hear the garage door opening. Sometimes I even amaze myself with my precise timing.

Chapter 7

THE PARKING LOT where I first met Marcus Christopher is similar to all my other favored locations. It's within a ninety-minute drive from my house, it happens to be in a camera blindspot, and it's near a place that wouldn't arouse suspicion. For this meeting, I want to make sure I give myself ample coverage and safety. Second meetings with the same client always have the potential to be even more dangerous. The second meeting is the second chance for a client to plan ahead. This means they're more likely to try recording meetings, involve police, or remember details of my appearance.

For this reason, I don't head straight to the meeting location. Instead, I take my car to a bar just down the street from the meeting spot forty-five minutes before our go time. I park directly under a street light as close to the door as I can get. I run my hands through my hair, fluffing up the blond locks just a little, making the kind of hairstyle that gets noticed and remembered. I slap on a little lip gloss for the same reason. Then, I make my way into the small bar. I count fifteen people spread out around the bar as I make my way to the only empty stool at the counter. I perch myself on it and order a whiskey on the rocks. "I haven't had a drink in over a year," I tell the bartender. I use that flirty voice every woman has, the one most of us loathe using. The one I only break out when absolutely necessary. The bartender smiles.

I sip the whiskey slowly, forcing myself to get louder and more boisterous halfway through the drink. "Is this stronger than it used to be?" I shout at the bartender.

He shakes his head. "Same stuff. You want a second one?"

"Better not." I finish the glass and check my watch. It's taken me about fifteen minutes to drink this, which is perfect. The last sip is smooth and makes me smile. Then I drop the glass on the bar and make a whooping noise. The guy next to me actually applauds. I fully engage the drunk girl routine, blinking too many times before I attempt speech. "I think I better walk around a little before I drive," I say. I'm careful not to oversell it —no slurring of the speech. I'm going for tipsy, not pass-out wasted.

"You want a coffee?" Bartender asks.

I rub my eyes a little, like I'm freshening up. "No. No, I had one whiskey. I'm good. I just want to walk a little."

His eyebrows go up. "Lady, it's dark out there. Are you sure that's the best idea?"

I nod slowly, letting my head lilt a little to the left on the way down. "If I'm still not in my best frame of mind after a quick stroll around in the cold, then you can get me a coffee." I actually hand him my car keys. "I'll be back for these in a little bit."

He stares at the keys for a second. I wonder if he's going to accept this offer or not. Bartenders are wildcards. Sometimes they're the best allies because they remember faces really well. That, as it turns out, is also their biggest threat to me and what I do for a living.

Finally, he reaches up and wraps his hand around the keys. "Be safe."

I keep up the drunk routine with a little wobbling on the way to the door. By the time I've left the parking lot, wound my way down the forest road a little ways, and can see the grocery store, I drop the act. The grocery store is only a good meeting place on Wednesday nights because that is the night the stocking crew stays late to work. Their cars are all in the back lot, and the lights will be on. One more car will not raise suspicion. Even one with people inside it can be explained away because people will assume we're employees on a break. It's perfect.

The car is in the exact same parking spot the client used the last time. I open the passenger side door, noting that it is free from most trash and recently wiped down. I shut the door and turn on my anger. "You want to tell me who took that picture?" I ask. My voice has a dangerous edge to it, but I keep it controlled. I'm not a hysterical woman; I'm an actual threat.

"I could ask you the same thing," Marcus Christopher counters.

I lean across the center console, bringing my face closer to his. "You already know what I can do. If you are threatening me, you know what I will do. Think about it. Plain and simple." I stick my hand in the pocket of my black jacket, and his eyes follow my hand.

His hands shoot up in front of him even as he leans away from me. "I didn't take it. I certainly didn't send it to you. I didn't even have an email address for you until you reached out to me. I swear."

I lean back just a little, but I keep my hand buried in my pocket. "If you didn't take it, and I didn't take it, we have a problem. Who knew you would be here?"

His eyes go wide as if he hadn't considered this possibility before. Amateur. "No one," he mumbles.

I sit all the way back and sigh. "I can dig into this; I have people. But it will cost money and time. Plus, if I find whoever took this picture..." I let the words hang in the air.

"I can't have this coming back to me." He reaches up and tugs on his hair. "Oh, God. What if this comes back to me?"

"Relax. I can take care of it. I assume you're paying?" I hold out my hand.

"How much will that cost?"

I make it look as though I'm thinking. "I'm not sure." I frown at him, hoping he can see the facial expression in the light coming in the front window. "This is a bigger ask than last time. What is your freedom worth, Marcus?"

"Fuck." He reaches below his seat and pulls out cash, exactly like I knew he would. Three bundles come out with him. But I see another one under there, peaking out. "This is all I have," he says as he thrusts the thirty thousand dollars at me.

"That's unfortunate because this will take at least forty." I take the cash. "I suppose we can make arrangements for you to pay the rest. I can have someone visit you at the new office in a week to pick it up." I turn my eyes to him, trying to look sweet. "One week is enough time for you to get the rest together, right?"

"You can't come to the office. Shit." He hands me the

other bundle. "Take it. Make this go away."

"Pleasure doing business with you, Marcus."

I slam the car door and head back the way I came. The night is cool; I can feel the air hitting my bare arms as I walk. It really would be enough to wake the drunk out of my other persona, I note. I should have no problem convincing this bartender that I took a quick stroll in the cold air and sobered up. A perfectly believable alibi, if one turns out to be needed. Of course, judging by Marcus Christopher's emphasis on the fact that this needs to disappear, it won't be needed.

I walk back to the bar quickly and smile when I see the blue sedan with the AC7 license plate in the parking lot. My second reason for choosing this location is falling into place perfectly. I make a quick stop at my own car to drop the bundles of cash, stored in the waistband of my jeans, under my own driver's seat. Then I lock the car manually and walk back into the bar.

When I pull open the door, I make my way directly to the bartender, all traces of the drunk act erased. "Hi there. Did you miss me?" I ask him.

He smiles and reaches under the counter to retrieve my keys, which he offers with a closed fist. "You want another whiskey to go with these?" he asks. "You seem like it's all run out of your system."

I turn my head, looking around the room. There, in a booth, nestled awfully close together, are Christina Montenegro and her gym rat, who happens to own that blue sedan in the parking lot.

I drop onto the stool. "I think that's a great idea." I pull a ten-dollar bill out of my wallet and drop it onto the counter. He pours the whiskey, takes the bill, and smiles at me. "Keep the change," I tell him. He winks and walks away.

I turn on my stool, aiming my legs at the pool table like I'm interested in the game two overweight guys in terrible clothing are playing. Really, the couple is at the edge of my vision from this angle.

I watch them kiss a little. I watch him snake his hand below the table, doing something that eventually makes Christina throw her head back and close her eyes. This lasts for a few seconds. Then she shoves him, hard. He slips along the booth and whispers something to her. She shoves him again. He shakes his head, gets up, and leaves the bar. She follows.

I like to plan things. I plan reconnaissance. I plan meetups. I plan deaths. But I also know one of the most important things when it comes to taking a life without getting caught is the story. If you can show the investigators a story that is believable, they'll take it. With that thought in mind, I slam back the last of my whiskey and stand up. I nod at the bartender. "Thank you."

"Come back anytime," he says with another wink.

Not likely, I think. You're going to remember my face, so it's to my advantage not to let you see it again.

I head outside, my keys already up so I look less suspicious. The mark and her lover are arguing in front of the blue sedan. I pay attention to their body language. She has her shoulders rolled back and her arms at her sides, looking almost casual except for the fact that her entire body is cocked and ready for a fight. His arms are crossed, and he's staring at the ground. This confirms my suspicions that she is the aggressive one.

"You didn't have to try and turn it into a fucking blow job in a dirty bathroom," she yells. I notice she takes a step closer to him, and he seems to shrink further into himself, rolling his shoulders inward and arching his back.

He mumbles something that may involve the word "trying." I can't be sure because he's facing away from me and speaking at a much lower volume than she is.

They're clearly not paying attention to me, so I allow myself to freeze, not actually moving closer to the car.

"It's always about you," she shouts again. "If I wanted that shit, I'd just fuck Thomas."

"Bitch." That one was clear. Even my eyes go wide. Boyfriend grew a spine pretty quickly.

Christina takes two quick steps and leans into him. This time, she drops her voice, but I think she says, "What did you just call me?" It's what I would ask.

He unwraps his arms and holds them out. "I'm sorry." His voice is louder, more normal. "We're both saying things we don't mean." He glances back toward the bar. "And we're making a scene out here."

I start walking again, but slowly. I'm probably ten steps away from my car when she softens a little. He responds by starting to close his arms in a hug.

But she moves fast, her arm flying out and slapping him across the face. "Take me the fuck home. Now." She spins on her heel, drops into the passenger seat, and slams the door.

I cannot hide the smile that takes over my face. I think I'm seeing clearly how the story of poor Christina's death will go now.

Chapter 8

HENRY'S GREEN SEDAN is already in the garage when I push the button to open the heavy door. I park my own car behind him in the driveway, pull my hair back into a ponytail, and exit my car. As soon as I push open the heavy door to the entryway, the smell of Thai food fills my nostrils. When left to fend for himself in the kitchen, my husband is the kind of guy who dials amazing delivery. I cross the dining room and spot Henry standing in the kitchen with two glasses of wine in his hands. He's wearing a pair of lounge pants I bought for him last Christmas, sporting the capital B for the only sports team around here he actually supports. His hair is wet, telling me he spent the evening at the gym and showered when he got home. "Thirsty?" he asks, holding one glass out in my direction.

"I've never turned down wine from a handsome man before," I answer with a wink.

Henry steps closer, and I take the wine glass from him. "Do handsome men often offer you wine?"

I take a big sip, letting the smell of wine replace the one of whiskey that would've coated my breath. "Just the same handsome man, on a semi-regular basis."

He leans in, kisses me deeply, then whispers. "I think he's just trying to get you into bed."

"Wine alone will not do that," I say. "But maybe if there were good food ..."

Henry laughs and steps back. "Hint taken. Let's eat first."

Behind him, I see the plates on the dining room table, still under the plastic domes from the restaurant. "It should still be hot," he says. "I got you that pad thai one with the shrimp you like."

I drop into the chair and take the lid off the container. The smell wafts up to my nose and makes my stomach growl. "I'm sorry I had to meet someone. Thanks for ordering dinner."

"No problem. Did the client meeting work out the way you'd hoped?" he asks.

I think of the money stashed under my driver's seat and smile. "Exactly the way I'd hoped. We're going to do a little business together, and I'm going to make a lot of money for it."

"Perfect. This is someone you've worked with before, right?" he asks.

Do I sense skepticism in my husband's expression? I dial up the innocence and lay on the technical talk. "Yeah, it's a local company based outside of Boston. The first time I worked with him, I was able to get through the firewall and access some employee files. That's dangerous because it could give me access to an inside man. Plus, if I can get employee files, who knows what else I would get with a bit more digging? So he wants me to add in some layers of security. Today's meeting was talking about my plan for the addition, how much time and money I think this will all take. It was three guys in suits and little old me. I don't think they expected me to have the answers that would work for them." I take a bite of my dinner and wash it down with wine. "I almost wish you'd been there to see the look on their faces when I started talking technical jargon."

"It's the blond hair," Henry says with a hint of laughter in his voice. "They expect you to be a vacant soccer mom."

I pretend to be shocked by this information, laying my hand across my chest and widening my eyes. "That's what they think? Maybe I should stop dyeing my hair." In truth, I know that's what people think. It's the reason I continue to make my hair this color when I go to the salon. Besides, Henry likes it.

He laughs. "You love throwing people's preconceived expectations in their faces, and you know it."

It's true. I do. Despite the fact that this man before me knows nothing of my double life, he knows more about me than anyone. He can read deep into my soul with just a single glance. When he's not here, I worry that I'm keeping too much from him. I worry that he can never truly know me because of this one piece of my life he's missing. But when he's here, it becomes obvious that I have nothing to fear. He knows who I really am deep down, even if he doesn't know details.

I get out of my chair and make my way around the table until I'm standing beside Henry. I push on the back of his chair, sliding it out across the wooden floor. He widens his eyes but says nothing. He even stays quiet and lets me pull down the lounge pants. He lets me take total control of the situation right there at the dining room table while the food cools.

Chapter 9

I SPEND THE next seven days gathering more information on Christina Montenegro and her patterns. There are a lot of people in her circle who seem aware of the affair. There's also a handful who seem aware of her pattern of abuse. The boyfriend's name turns out to be Patrick Lander. I can't find anything, other than sleeping with a married woman, that tells me he's a terrible guy. That means I need to be more careful. Pining this all on him with my story would be convenient, but it doesn't feel right.

So, instead, I settle on this story.

Christina Montenegro is a serial abuser of men. She regularly hits both her husband and her boyfriend. Investigators dig into her past and find evidence of this, including a broken wrist in Patrick's past and a questionable car accident in Thomas'.

For the last three years, patterns tell us Christina has been escalating. Friends report that the fighting has become more "constant" and "erratic." A coworker makes mention that Patrick is considering "cutting his losses" at work one day, and Christina loses it.

She stops on the way home from work at a local hardware store, where she is caught on camera making a purchase with cash. The clerk doesn't remember what she bought, only that she was there. Later, a cash receipt for the same hardware store and a box of rat poisoning are found in her trash can, leading investigators to conclude that was the item purchased.

Later that same night, a Thursday, Christina cooks dinner at her house for Patrick while Thomas is out late. According to Patrick, the two ate the chili, and each had one glass of wine. He says the fighting did not begin until the meal was finished and it was time to clean up. Patrick explains that the argument was over whether Patrick should clean up because Christina cooked or whether they should save the clean up for later and enjoy their time alone without Thomas.

Patrick says it was around this time that he started to feel sick and decided to go home. Around 3 AM, Patrick got up to use the restroom and had blood in his urine. He called an ambulance. At the hospital, he was tested for foreign substances, and they found evidence of an anti-coagulant in high levels. Patrick is not on blood thinners, but they are an active ingredient in rat poisoning. Patrick was admitted and treated. He expressed concern for his associate from work, Christina, who he had recently shared a meal with.

Police arrived at the residence of Christina and Thomas Montenegro at 6:15 AM on Friday morning to do a well visit. Thomas explains that his wife hadn't been feeling well and is soaking in the bathtub. He knocks on the door, attempting to draw her attention. When there is no answer, he opens the bathroom door.

Christina is found in the tub, which is full of bloody water. Christina does not have a pulse. Attempts to resuscitate her are unsuccessful. She is pronounced dead when the coroner arrives on scene at 6:48 AM.

Autopsy will reveal high levels of blood thinner and a cut on her calf, which appears to be caused by a razor blade. A woman's razor was found in the bottom of the tub. An empty container of rat poison was found in the garbage can. Traces of the poison, which does contain a blood thinner, were found in the chili, leftovers of which were in a container in the refrigerator.

It is the belief of the investigators that Christina Montenegro, whether intentionally or accidentally, put rat poisoning in the food she was cooking. The fact that the container for the poison made it to the trash leads investigators to believe it was intentional, perhaps as an effort to poison Patrick Lander. However, the fact that she ingested it herself leads us to believe it was some kind of accident.

Either way, Christina Montenegro did not die simply from ingesting the poison. She could have been treated at the hospital, like Patrick was. It appears she nicked her leg with a razor while shaving. At that point, the blood thinners caused her to bleed out.

The homicide detectives assigned to the case rule the death as accidental.

Not a bad story, right? Perhaps you're wondering how I pulled this all off? Well, I enjoy bragging, and I rarely get to do it. So, let me explain.

Christina went grocery shopping on Wednesday afternoon when she got off work. When she brought her groceries in through the garage, she left it open. That was my opportunity to head into the garage and use a handheld electric screwdriver to back out the top two screws of each L-bracket on a shelf holding paint cans. Later that night, although I wasn't there to witness the effect, the bottom two screws on the shelf would fail and snap at the head from the pressure.

This is how Christina ended up at the hardware store across the street from the gym where she works, buying a box of screws and wall anchors. They come in a box about the size of a walkman from the 1980s and cost $9.99. Do you know what else comes in a box that size and has that exact price point? A box of rat poison at the same store. Coincidentally, that is what I bought. I got in line behind Christina, which put us at the two side-by-side registers at basically the same time. We both paid cash and dropped our receipts into the cute little plastic bag emblazoned with the hardware store logo.

Thursday night, Christina invited Patrick to dinner. This one was trickier for me to get the timing right on because Christina keeps her blinds closed when she is home alone. I ended up waiting near the exterior wall for her bathroom so I could hear when the shower turned on. I took this opportunity to enter through a window at the back of the house, drop the rat poisoning into the chili and give it a little stir, and go back out the same window. I dropped the hardware store bag, with the cash receipt and the empty box in the exterior trash can. Practically gift-wrapped for the investigator.

The rest of it really was exactly as the police saw it, which is perfect. Now I wouldn't have been above returning to the house to give her a small cut myself. I knew the effects of the active ingredient in the poison. I knew any decent-sized cut would be enough. My plan was, originally, to give her a cut on the hand while she was in the kitchen. This would make it look as though she had been preparing another meal. I was planning on waiting for Thomas to leave for work, in case she screamed when she saw me.

It really worked out for me that she decided to try shaving her legs and cut herself.

So, lots of planning and planting evidence ended with something that surprised even me. But I'm sure you still think I'm the monster in this scenario. That's fine, but just remember something: Patrick is going to be fine. If anything, the lack of regular fights and violence with Christina is going to be an improvement for him. He's the winner in all of this.

Chapter 10

———◆———

SATURDAY NIGHT, THE plan is to take things easy. I get rid of the burner cell phone I was using and don't bother to replace it right away. I call a local restaurant we really like and order two of their filet mignon meals with scalloped potatoes and Brussels sprouts, which they cook in bacon fat. I also order their most expensive bottle of red wine and a decadent butter cake dessert. I tell them to have it all delivered by 6 PM.

Henry and I settle onto the couch in the family room, snuggled together under a thin blanket. "What would you like to watch tonight?" he asks, remote in hand.

"Something brainless," I answer. "I don't want to have to think too deeply about what is happening."

He laughs. "No thinking. Got it." He scrolls through the preview tiles on the screen slowly as if waiting for me to stop him. I almost laugh when he pauses for a full two-count on the show about the forensic pathologist who is also a serial killer. We've watched quite a few episodes of this man brutally murdering only bad people. I swear that show was his idea, not mine.

But tonight, Henry keeps scrolling, perhaps deciding

that a thriller requires too much brain power. The second time he stops, it's on a show with an added laugh track that features a couple of average-intelligence parents raising a group of genius children. "How about this one?" he asks.

"Perfect." I nestle into him, my head resting on his chest, and enjoy the show. We manage to sneak in two full episodes before the doorbell rings, and my phone alerts me my no-contact delivery has arrived.

Henry hits pause. I get up to retrieve the food while he retrieves silverware, wine glasses, and napkins from the other room. I set up the food on the coffee table while Henry pours the wine. "This smells amazing," he says.

I take a big whiff. "That may be the desert you're smelling."

Henry shakes his head. "Butter cake is your weakness. Mine is beef." As if to prove his point, he cuts a generous slice of his steak and chews slowly. I laugh out loud when his eyes slip closed, apparently from the ecstasy of the experience.

He opens his eyes, now full of their own kind of laughter, and tips his head toward the TV. "What do you think? Should we finish the episode?"

Our coffee table is just far enough away from the couch to make it awkward to stretch for it when you're eating in here, so I drop onto the floor, pulling my feet underneath me. "Ready," I tell him.

He hits play, and we eat while laughing our way through the show.

I push my plate back just about the time the third episode is ending. "Well," I tell him, "this is unfortunate."

"What is?"

"I'm too full for butter cake." I pout at the small box still sitting untouched on the corner of the table. "Which is a tragedy."

"I do know one fun way to burn some calories." Henry waggles his eyebrows at me. Then, in case I wasn't sure what he was implying, he leans in to give me a passionate kiss. I don't even pretend to argue. I let my perfect husband peel my clothes off my body and burn calories with him in the perfect way.

He pulls the blanket off the couch and over our naked bodies when we are both satisfied. "Do you think you have room for dessert now?" he asks.

"One more episode, and then I'm devouring that cake."

He kisses me on the forehead as he reaches for the remote. "We really do have the perfect life, don't we?" he asks.

It's a rhetorical question that he doesn't need me to answer. Still, I smile at him and offer my opinion. "Perfect in every way."

We move back to the comfort of the couch while we share our dessert. Then we forget the dessert as we fall into a second round of passionate sex. We eventually fall asleep on the couch with the TV still playing in the background. At some point in the middle of the night, darkness the only thing on the other side of our curtains, I wake up. I smile at my husband, reach for the remote, and flip off the TV. Then I settle deeper into his arms and allow myself to fall back to dreamland.

Sunday morning, I get up and head out to the little store in the center of town. Basically, this store is the kind you'd never believe still exists if you didn't have one in your neighborhood. It's a small wooden building that has been here in our town for well over one hundred years. The front of the building is essentially a convenience store, although the kind that still has a candy counter selling loose candy sticks for a penny a piece. The back is a row of post office boxes that anyone can rent.

I wave at the proprietor on my way back to the boxes. I check the one for Regina and Henry King first, taking out three bills and a handful of flyers. I keep these in my left hand as I walk my way over to the box rented to Rachel Kingston. From this one, I remove one envelope and a small box. These, I throw into the purse slung over my shoulder.

I make my way back out to the store, grabbing a loaf of bread and a half gallon of milk. At the register, I make sure to set my mail down on the counter so the nosey proprietor can see it. He once asked me if I checked someone else's box back there; his tone of voice indicated he was joking, but I'm careful to make sure he sees the mail all has my name now. This little old man, with his cap of white hair, offers me a smile. "You both doing well?" he asks.

I nod. "How about you and yours?"

"As good as can be expected," he answers. He pushes the milk back across the counter to me and gives me my total. I hand him a ten dollar bill and wait while he slowly counts out the change. We have the same exact interaction, word-for-word, almost every time I'm in this store. It's part of my routine. He drops the change into my hand. "Be safe," he says.

"You as well." It's like a script, and I don't deviate from it.

When we're done, I grab the mail and head out to my car. I drop the groceries, my purse, and the mail on the passenger seat and slowly back out of the parking spot. I am always careful. I always assume I am being watched.

I wait until I come to a full stop at a stoplight about a mile from the store. Then, I finally pull the small box from my purse and slice open the seal with my thumbnail. The prepaid burner phone falls out of the box and into my hand, exactly as I knew it would.

I don't talk about this much because I like having the power, but I do have a handler who helps make sure all my deals go through. It's basically like having an assistant. He orders my burner phones, deals with any clients that are truly pressuring me, and reminds me if I have something big coming up that I may have forgotten about. I have no idea what his name is, and I only pay him a monthly stipend. I've often considered turning my investigative skills to finding out who he is, but I haven't done it yet. Honestly, if any of our interactions ever gave me bad vibes, I'd do it. But for now, he's happy with the arrangement, and so am I.

I take a left turn into a local elementary school, closed because of the weekend, and park near the dumpster. I leave the car running but hop out and toss the box addressed to Rachel Kingston into the dumpster. The lid slams with an echoing finality when I drop it. Back in my car, it's another simple left-hand turn to put me back on the road to my house.

I'm back at the house, in front of the computer, working on trying to hack into another medical firm over an hour later when the new burner phone comes to life, vibrating across the desk.

I flip it open and put it to my ear. "Hello."

"Hi, there." The voice on the other end of the line is male. He is also remarkably cheery, considering the kind of clientele who normally call me.

"When can you meet?"

"Shouldn't we discuss what we're meeting about?"

Red flags start popping up in my mind. He's too relaxed. He's trying to get me to talk more than I like to. Could this man be an undercover detective? How did he get this information?

"When can you meet?" I repeat. I'm already opening an incognito browser to send off an email to my handler.

"Now, now. Let's take it easy here. You're not exactly in the line of being trustworthy, considering what I know you do for a living. How can I be sure it's safe for me to—" I hang up the phone before he can finish the sentence.

I don't get intimidated. I don't get roped into situations that are dangerous for me. I'm too careful for that. In the email box, I type, *I'm going to need a new phone again. This one is compromised. Rush delivery—I'll pay for it. Take it from the account.*

The account that my handler has access to has just around a hundred thousand dollars in it at all times. With my permission, this is the account from which he makes his own monthly withdrawal. It keeps things simple.

I hold the power button down until the burner phone vibrates in my hand, a signal that it is powering down. Then I toss it into my shoes, resting by the door to my bedroom. Later, I'll take it out and throw it into the local river reservoir.

With the phone off, I don't feel a pressing need to take care of it immediately. I can take my time and get some more of my work done. I do eye the phone once more, just to be sure it is off. It lies there like a dead mouse, waiting for me to dispose of the carcass.

This doesn't happen often, a call that I don't take. But anyone who breaks my rules ends up like this. I control the situation; I say when, I say how. If anything doesn't feel right, I remind myself I don't need the money and move on. In this line of work, you can never be too careful.

Chapter 11

I SIT DOWN in front of the computer three days later and move the Montenegro file from my in-progress folder to my blackmail possibility folder. As is my procedure, I will leave this file alone now for anywhere from three to six months, depending on how the investigation goes and how much heat I think is on. Then I will either make a move on it or delete it altogether.

Currently, the only other file in the blackmail folder that has a date far enough out to focus on is the one for Marcus Christopher, my client in the dark car, who has now paid me an additional forty thousand dollars to handle the photograph he believes someone sent me. I open a secure email window. It would be reasonable to assume I would've come home from the meeting with Mr. Christopher and immediately started my research to try and find the source of the photograph. Then, assuming I had nothing else on my plate, I could have handled the person who supplied the file the following day. Therefore, it is entirely reasonable to assume I am safe to tell the client that the situation is handled. I could move him out of my case files altogether and let him go from my life. He's been punished enough, I think, for his part in all this. It's time to cut him loose.

But for some reason, the email feels like a bad move. Marcus Christopher was a jumpy man when last we met. Jumpy men have a tendency to make a knee-jerk phone call to authorities or to let something slip to a family member. I need him to not be afraid of the nameless person who took the photograph, so it's important to reassure him that it's handled. I do, however, want him to continue to fear me. Fear of me will keep him from doing something stupid to put me in danger.

I close the email window and reach for a plain four-by-six-inch white index card from the pile on my desk. Using an average ballpoint pen, I simply write on the card, *Everything has been handled as we discussed.* I don't sign it.

I open Marcus Christopher's file and retrieve the address for his new place of employment. I commit it to memory and close the file again. With a quick drag, I move the entire file to a folder marked 'Completed.'

Then I put my shoes on, grab my purse, and head for my car. On the way out the front door, I shoot a text message to Henry. *Afternoon looks really light. I'm heading to town to run a few errands. Need anything at the store?*

I lock the front door, use my remote to unlock my car, and drop into the driver's seat. Before I can even turn the key, my phone dings with a response from Henry. *Something chocolate for dessert would be delicious.*

Consider it done, I reply. Then I pull my car out of the driveway and head toward town. First stop, new disposable phone. The last one, of course, found itself in the bottom of the local water reservoir two days ago.

The post office box for Regina and Henry King is empty

this time around. I find only the disposable cell phone package in the other box. I toss that package into my purse and spin back into the main store. I wave at the little old man behind the register. "Nothing in my box today," I tell him. "I guess I'll see you tomorrow."

"Have a good one," he calls back.

Since I'm buying nothing, there's no reason to get closer to him at the counter. No reason for him to notice the package stuffed in my purse or ask any questions. Sometimes it just works out.

I head further into town next, parking about a quarter of a mile away from Marcus Christopher's new employer. Locking my car, I take the remaining distance on foot. While I walk, I unwrap and power on the new phone. I toss the garbage into trash cans I pass along the way, always grateful for small towns' obsessions with putting garbage cans everywhere to keep trash off the street.

I turn into the business that looks more like an old house and approach a young woman sitting at a desk. "Hi. Can you give this message to Marcus for me?" I ask her, handing her a small envelope containing only the index card.

"He's here," she tells me. "You're welcome to head back there and give it to him yourself."

"No, thanks," I answer, wrinkling my nose. "I'd honestly rather not see him if that's alright with you. Just give him the envelope."

"Who should I tell him it's from?" she asks as I'm already turning to walk out.

"He'll know." I tell her. I'm out the door before she can even bellow his name, although I think I hear her do that through the wooden front door.

I cross the street and stand, leaning on a light post, staring at the house. In my head, I'm counting to two hundred. I figure if I reach two hundred and he hasn't come out to see who dropped off the envelope, I'll just head for my car and go home.

At one hundred eighty seven, the door of the business opens, and Marcus Christopher steps out onto the porch. From my location across the street, I wave. I'm far enough away to miss the fear I imagine is all over his face, but I do see him redden slightly before he ducks back into the office.

I'm halfway back to my car, fantasizing about what sort of chocolate I might get at the store, when the phone rings in my pocket. I fish it out and flip it open. "Hello?"

"I was told to call you if I had the money for your services." A young woman, some strength behind her voice. Either she's completely sure of herself, or she's done some practicing before calling me. She sounds composed and ready. I like her right away.

"Can you meet tonight?" I ask.

"Whatever works for you," she answers. It's the right answer.

"Great. 7:15 tonight. Worcester Art Museum. Stand on the steps off Lancaster Street at the railing. Face out away from the building. Look like you're enjoying the sunset. Maybe snap a picture of it if you feel the need to, although I won't approach you while your phone is out. Wait for me to join you. I'll comment on the sunset."

"Got it," she says with the confidence of someone who has a good memory for details. She's not writing this down, but I feel confident she'll get it right.

"Bring cash and a picture."

"See you then." She is actually the first to hang up, which doesn't happen to me often.

I snap the phone closed and slip it in my pocket. I should have plenty of time to get the dessert, put dinner in the oven, and then give Henry some excuse about meeting a client. I can meet up with this girl, get myself another job, and be home in time to eat a little of the dinner and then plenty of that chocolate I buy.

By the time I've reached the car, I've decided I'm going for a chocolate mousse cake. It'll be perfect.

Chapter 12

THAT NIGHT I head to the Lutheran church on Lancaster Street and park my car in their parking lot. I have no idea where my potential new client may be parked, but the Art Museum is closed at this time of night, so it would be suspicious if both of us parked in the same otherwise empty lot. The church, however, runs events in the evenings and will have people coming and going.

I get out of my car and walk around, smiling to myself when I see a single woman standing on the steps of the museum. She's younger than I expected, young enough to make me think life hasn't had a chance to beat her up yet. This makes me think if life hasn't done it, someone likely has. I hate cases like that, but money is money.

I wait for her to slip her cell phone, which she was using to take pictures of the sunset, into her pocket before I make my way across the street and up the stairs to her. I stand directly beside her, looking the same way she is looking. "Beautiful sunset tonight," I remark.

I notice her face registers shock at my appearance. "Are you ..." She stops herself, shakes her head. "Sorry. No questions."

"No questions," I agree. "Just yes or no answers to my questions." I keep my gaze forward as if I'm more interested in the lowering sun than I am in this young lady. "You are aware of what I do?"

Yes.

The meeting goes off without a hitch. She hands me a purse full of thirty thousand dollars and the envelope I need. Normally, I allow myself to wait at least twelve hours before I get started, but something about this client's sweet face and her age make me curious enough to start while Henry is at the gym. I decide I'll just get a little work done, enough to satiate my curiosity for the night.

I immediately begin digging into her past. The man she wants me to take out, at first, appears to have absolutely no connection to her. In fact, I'm not even sure how she already knew about him. The man has been in the state for only about a month. Previously, he was living down south, literally hundreds of miles away.

Digging a little deeper, I find that she spent a few years back in her elementary school days in that same state. It's times like this that I'm almost tempted to reach out to clients again. Then I remember the "no more contact" rule is as much for my safety as theirs. I can't give them a second chance to remember my face without a really good reason. Normally, money is the only reason good enough. I keep digging.

I find an old church bulletin with a version of his name in it. I was told his name is William, and this lists him as Bill.

Common enough nickname means it's probably him. The old church flyer mentions his outreach program with an elementary school. This, of course, was over fifteen years ago.

Still, I'm able to track the district information through old newspapers. There is mention of a scandal involving a volunteer suspected of impropriety. No details are given. The article assures the community that children are being offered counseling if necessary.

A bad feeling roots in my stomach, and I find myself clenching my jaw. I close my eyes, push away from the computer, and take a deep breath. Some cases get to me more than others. Some people just feel inherently more evil than others. I take two more deep breaths before I allow myself to get back to work. Don't assume anything, I tell myself. Find the story.

Two hours later, I have proof that my client was a student at that elementary school. I can't find any proof that she may have interacted with the mark. What I can find is that her parents had meetings with the school, she was withdrawn within two months of the newspaper article, and the family moved to Massachusetts where she still resides. Once in the new state, I suspect she was also receiving some kind of emotional counseling, as her parents liked and followed a child and family therapy center about six months after the move. It's possible they only looked it into, but it's also possible she received treatment.

I push back from the computer again and sigh. If I had to guess, which I often find myself needing to do at this stage in the game, I'd bet on the school district having a complaint from these parents. I would imagine it was nothing they could prove, since I can't find evidence charges were ever filed. I certainly hope it wasn't sexual because I'd like to think the school would've fought harder for that. Whatever it was, this child had to leave the state to get away from those memories.

She grew up here, away from that past. She went to college and earned herself a degree. She now counsels children at a local school, with a local church, and through the foster system. She lives alone in a great community in a nice place. She is well respected and handles her social media presence well. Not at all my typical clientele. So what changed in her life?

By all appearances, it all changed with one major thing. The mark is now in Massachusetts.

I can't imagine the pain she must have felt when she found him. Calling me and paying me thirty thousand dollars must have been her only option. Now I feel guilt, which happens sometimes. This young lady is a counselor herself. She doesn't get paid much, I'm sure. This money must be everything she has to her name.

I pick up the picture she gave me. The man is older, sporting gray hair and a beer gut that comes from a life of comfort. What has he been up to for all these years? That seems like a really important question—one that may make my decision for me.

I'm startled when I hear the garage door rolling up. I quickly close down everything, clear the history, and open the files for my day job. With my left hand, I shove the picture of the mark under the wireless keyboard. I don't bother rubbing the strain out of my eyes or trying to look more alert. On the contrary, I actually lean into the screen and get started trying to hack into the server for the newest company to hire my legitimate services.

Henry comes into the room and lays his hand on my shoulder. I jolt a little from the surprise. "What time is it?" I ask, glancing down at the clock in the corner of the screen.

"Time for me to whip up something for us to snack on, I think. You look like this might be an all-nighter." He plants a quick kiss on my forehead. "Think you'll be ready for a break in about fifteen minutes?"

"I can stop now," I start pushing back the rolling chair.

Henry stops me with a firm hand. "Stay here. I'll make some late night grilled cheese sandwiches."

I can't believe I let the evening get away from me digging into this new client. It's unprofessional, and it could have blown everything. I needed to get a little work done today for this new company, and I blew that as well. I let my shoulders sag. "That would actually be really helpful. I just need ten more minutes."

"Perfect." He gives me another kiss and leaves the room. "If the smoke alarm goes off, just ignore it."

"What if I hear sirens?" I ask, my tone playful.

Henry's laugh echoes back up the hallway and into the room. "Don't ignore those."

I turn my attention back to the computer and start working on the server again. When I hear Henry banging around in the kitchen, opening and closing cabinets, I get up and put the photograph in a safe place. Then I drop back into the chair and really focus.

By the time Henry pops back into the doorway to tell me my sandwich is ready, I've found a weakness I can exploit. I finish off an email to the company explaining that the weakness will require more investigation and attach my bill.

Then I retire to spend more time with my husband.

Comfort food, handsome company, and no thoughts about some guy who may or may not have harassed a young girl while he was volunteering at an elementary school fifteen years ago make for a perfect evening.

Chapter 13

—◆—

Regina,
Thank you for finding the flaw in our system. We have spoken to the security team, and they are capable of plugging the hole on our end. Please see the proposed amended invoice (attached). We will not need you to handle the fix, but we would like to offer you an additional contract in one week to try again to gain access to the server. You'll notice we are also including a $1300 bonus for finding the flaw. To accept the new contract, simply sign and return before close of business Friday.

I ACTUALLY LAUGH out loud to the empty room at the email. Why these companies continue to think their own teams can handle these things is beyond me. But I already know how this will play out. They'll pay me my normal fee to try again next week; I'll still be able to get in because the weakness will still be there. Then we'll repeat all this. From my end, that is the definition of easy money.

I use my software to include my digital signature and drop the new document into an email reply. *Sounds good, thank you. I will begin my new attempt to access the server exactly seven days from today unless I hear otherwise.*

Beside me the prepaid phone vibrates. I hit send on the email and put the flip phone up to my ear. "Hello?"

"Hello?" Male voice. The questioning tone could be an indication of second thoughts.

"When can you meet?" I ask.

"Anytime, really. Tomorrow would be good."

"Today would be better," I respond. If he is hesitating, he may back out if I give him too long. Then I've wasted a drive to a location and didn't get any cash for my time. Backing out is bad news, unless they do it after I've been paid.

"I guess I could do that. Maybe if it was this afternoon and was near my work."

Oh, I don't like that. I control the places, and I don't want personal information fed to me by someone who may be lying. I prefer to do all my own research.

"Could you get to the Framingham Amtrak station today?" I offer one of my central locations, one that wouldn't require me to ask him where he works. I pull up the schedule for the train station on my computer, looking for a time when it would be busy. I want a time near a train arrival or departure that would have the area full of people.

"I can do that but I have to be back as soon as I can. Can we make it in about forty-five minutes?"

I scroll up on the schedule. That works. If I leave now I can make it there in forty. "Done. Park in the handicap spot near the pull out for the 135 right by the sign for the 126. If that spot is full, wait for it." I specifically choose that spot because it's never full. It's a handicap spot that makes no sense because it's not a convenient distance from anything. "Keep the doors unlocked but the car turned off and the windows up."

"Right, I was told that. I was also told—"

"Bring cash." I hang up the phone. That person was

dangerously close to trying to take charge of this meeting. I don't like meeting in broad daylight, and I don't like clients who try to take charge. I will need to be on my guard today. If there are any more red flags from this client, I'm out.

For this meeting, my all black get-up will not work. That is an outfit designed to handle night time meetups. I jog upstairs to our bedroom and my closet. For this meeting, I'm going to need to look the part of a day commuter, so I slip into a blue cotton dress with a wide white belt, the kind I would wear to a boring office job. I keep my blonde hair down and loose around my shoulders. I need to leave now if I'm going to make it on time, so I throw some shoes on and hurry out. If I'm lucky, traffic will be light.

I make decent time. When I arrive at the train depot, I park on the opposite side of the road, closer to the actual train. Then I wander, making it a point to look like I'm trying to find someone and their car. Sometimes selling the story is all about convincing your own brain it's true.

I sigh in exasperation when I've wandered the lot for a few minutes. Then, I pick my head up and aim it at the handicap spot across the busy road. I act excited, wave, and jog. There is a car in that spot and a man sitting inside the car. From this distance, he does look a little nervous.

I pull open the passenger door and drop into the seat beside him. There is a manilla envelope on the center console between us. He's not much older than me; if I had to guess, I'd call him mid-forties. He looks like he may work out a little but also enjoys fine meals. He's in that rich man's comfort zone, not overweight but not overly fit either. I shut the door.

"I do all the talking. You are only allowed to answer yes

or no. Understand?" I forgo my usual finger on the lips gesture because there are so many people around.

"Yes." He doesn't sound as nervous now as he did before.

"You are aware of what I do?"

His eyes widen. "Yes." He draws out the word as if it were a question.

I look him up and down. The nice, tailored suit that speaks of an office job. The watch on his wrist that looks expensive. The car itself, an Infiniti QX80 that the average working person cannot afford. "This is about someone from work?" I guess.

"No, but it has to look like an accident."

I pull away from the man a little, set my hand on the handle of the door. "You answer simple yes or no, or I'm leaving."

He nods his agreement but doesn't look particularly sorry.

"Is this about an acquaintance, then?" I ask again. He doesn't appear to be wearing a wedding ring.

"No."

I glance at the envelope. The rules are usually pretty simple. Either an earlier client or my handler will tell them to bring me one recent photograph of the mark with the full name of the mark. That is all that should be nestled in that envelope. It doesn't really matter to me who the person is to him. I only ask because I'm curious. Part of me, I think, enjoys guessing to shock them with how easy they are to read.

I bring my eyes back to his face, ready to make my offer. With the red flags, I need to come in high for this client. If he can't make that, we are done. "One hundred thousand," I tell him.

"It cannot be traceable back to me," he says. "No matter what."

I fling open the door beside me.

"I don't want people showing up at my–" That's all I hear because I've already slammed the expensive door shut behind me. It turns out when you pay for a high end car, it does a pretty decent job of keeping the sound inside the vehicle.

I walk back to my car quickly, listening for footsteps or his voice behind me. When I reach my car, I take the prepaid cell out of my purse and toss it in my hand a few times. Then I walk with the rest of the passengers toward the train platform. I stand beside the tracks, watching the train as it starts to move away. I wait until it is almost full speed before launching the phone down near the rails. My only regret is that I don't get to hear the crunch because the clacking is already so loud.

Chapter 14

IF I SAID the meeting at the station didn't bother me and consume my thoughts for the next few days, I'd be lying. It's the thing that keeps popping back up in my memory when I should be focusing on something else. There were definitely warning signs on the call, which is why I've trained myself to look for things like that. I didn't make a mistake; I'm confident in that. But I spend time trying to decide if there's anything I should be doing differently. Is there some new rule I should add?

I decide I did everything right. I took the meeting, I laid down the rules, and I left the meeting when things weren't going according to plan. The rules have served me well and, I decide, they protect me from idiots like this guy at the station. By the time my new cell phone arrives, I've put it out of my head completely to focus on the only current mark in my files. William Archer.

William Archer lives on the top floor of a three-level apartment complex. He has a western facing unit in the middle of two others. He comes and goes from this apartment in an old red Ford Bronco at random times of the day as if he doesn't have a schedule to follow. Besides regular trips to grocery stores, mostly for pre-packaged food, he seems to spend most of his time at a little bar. The only place he seems to go on a semi-regular schedule is a local church, which he visits most days of the week. He sits alone at the bar and at his house; I have never seen him with another person. Of course, there is one location that I haven't followed him into in all of my times dealing with him.

I'm thinking about William as I pull into my local grocery store parking lot, half an hour from his house or his routines. I park in a spot near the front and put the car in park, but I don't turn it off. My cell phone is resting on the center console beside me. I pick it up and thumb it open. Pulling up the privacy settings, I turn off location services. Then, I pull my car back out onto the main road and head toward William's town. Half an hour later, I pass the little bar he likes to frequent. I smile when I see his Bronco parked outside. That makes my next stop obvious.

Today is the day I get to visit the one location my mark likes to spend his time that I have yet to view. I turn down the little forest road, lined on both sides with trees, and drive until the building comes into sight. Seems like a good day for me to get a little more personal with William's new church.

I park my car in the back of the paved lot, closest to the road, and walk up toward the front door. I snap a few pictures on my phone, keeping up the image of someone who may be scoping out the church and appreciating its beauty. There are three other cars in the parking lot, all in the closest spaces to the entrance.

I notice a marquee at the foot of the entrance stairs and

make my way to it. This board has flyers for events being held at the church and times. I open my calendar app and use it to remember which days and times I've seen William be here instead of at the bar. This week it would've been Tuesday and Wednesday around three in the afternoon. Thursday, he was here briefly around eleven, then he left and returned at three. Friday, he was back at three.

I scope out the flyers. AA Meetings are held at night, and I've never seen William here at night. Couples counseling is by appointment; I suppose that could be what is happening. But my gut instinct is to throw this one out. William is not half of a couple, and I can't imagine him being entrusted to counsel other people who are. Grief circles meet on Tuesdays but not until five. He was definitely not here at five.

The last flyer, besides the one with regular service times for the church, is for Kids Kamp. I roll my eyes at the use of the K for kamp, which seems counterproductive when you're dealing with children who may or may not know that isn't how you spell the word. Kids Kamp is a "place for children and teens to come after school for about an hour a day to learn about the word of God." It's held Tuesday through Friday from three to four.

The same times I have seen William here.

My stomach clenches. This feels right for the schedule and somehow so wrong for the world. William, the volunteer who may have interacted with my client, is working with children again?

"Can I help you with something?" a woman asks. I look out around the board to find a woman standing on the top step. She's an older woman, the picture perfect image of the classic grandmother. She's wearing a black floral dress, her gray locks pulled into a severe bun, plain black flats, and a huge smile. Something about her instantly makes me feel warm and comforted.

I smile back at her. "I was just looking at what you offer here. I'm new to the community."

She takes a step toward me. "That's wonderful, dear. What kind of offerings are you interested in? We have a lovely church service twice on Sundays that allows you to pick the time more convenient for you and your family."

"I see that." I point toward the board. "That's wonderful, thank you." I take a few steps closer to her. "I also see that you have a children's group that meets after school. I love working with children. Are you looking for new volunteers to help with that?"

She frowns, briefly. "Well I can't just let anyone jump in to working with our children. I'm sure you understand."

"Of course." I chuckle a little, channeling my best suburban Mom impression. "I wouldn't be comfortable with the program if you did. I'm merely curious if something like that would even be an option if we were to choose this church as our own."

Can you choose a church as your own? It's the best language I could come up with under the circumstances.

Grandma smiles again, softer but comforting none-the-less. "I'm not sure, actually. I can take your name and ask Pastor Steve if you'd like. But I know he just brought Bill on board in the last month. I'm not sure he needs anyone new at this time."

Bingo. "No problem. I just like to be helpful. Maybe I'll pop in to see you this Sunday and talk to someone about it then."

"If you'll be here anyway, you could speak to Pastor Steve yourself. After the service you just come find me, and I'll introduce you. I'm easy to find, dear. I'll be the one playing the piano."

"Great, thank you." I turn and start to walk back to my car.

"Oh, I didn't get your name," the woman calls to me.

I reach into my purse and grab my cell phone, despite the fact that it didn't ring. I pull it up to my ear. "Hello?" I nod like I'm listening to someone. Then I mouth to the woman, "Sorry, I really have to take this" and point to my car.

I keep the phone up to my ear even as I pull out of the parking lot for the church. She watches me drive away, suspicion written all over her face. I almost feel bad for making her doubt me. I would feel worse if it wasn't for the fact that she gave me exactly what I needed.

That sweet little woman just confirmed Bill is working with children at that church. Why does that information give me a terrible feeling in my stomach?

Chapter 15

I PARK IN the grocery store parking lot and open my cell phone. The settings are already an open window since I accessed them earlier today. I scroll down to the privacy setting and turn my location services back on. Henry and I are on the same cell phone plan, and we have been known to use the location app to find each other in the past. Obviously, the church where Bill works is not someplace Henry would expect me to be. He would, however, expect me to be at a grocery store today.

When I parked here this morning and turned off the location services, it would have stopped sharing that location with Henry. I've done this with him nearby and checked his phone. It doesn't alert him that I've turned it off and, in the app, it continues to show my last location before it was turned off. If he's looking carefully, he'll notice it tells him it's been hours since my location changed. Lucky for me, he's not aware how long it takes to grocery shop. But I'm sure even he could figure out that it doesn't take the three hours I've been gone plus an additional hour for me to actually get the shopping list complete. Good thing I already thought of that.

I turn the car off and dial the number on the parking

space in front of me. The guy who answers sounds exhausted. Poor guy hates his job. "I'm here to pick up my order," I tell him.

"Name?"

"Regina King."

"What space did you park in?"

I check the sign. "3."

"I'll be out in a minute," he tells me. Then I hear the click that tells me he is gone.

I put the phone back in the center console and spin the radio dial up to enjoy a little music while I wait. Two songs later, an employee in a green vest comes out of the doors wheeling a cart full of bags. He heads straight for my car. I hit the unlock button, turn the radio back down, and roll down the window. "You can put them in the back, please," I tell him when he approaches.

He opens the back of the car and loads all the bags up. "You want the receipt back here or with you?" he asks.

"Back there is great, thank you."

"Yeah, whatever." He slams the lid of the trunk shut and stomps off to the entrance again, pushing his now empty cart.

There, three hours of grocery shopping later I've managed to get everything on my list. Sometimes, I'm brilliant.

I restart the car and turn onto the road. My phone rings, and I click the green answer button on the steering wheel. Henry's voice fills the car. "Hey, babe. Are you home?"

"No, I just finished at the grocery store. I'm on my way home. Maybe fifteen minutes away. Why, what's up?"

Henry groans in frustration. "We're having a computer problem here. I was hoping you could VPN in like you did that one time and see if you can find something."

I hit my turn signal and change lanes. "I'm honestly right downtown. I'm like five minutes from the bank. I'll just come there."

"What about the groceries?" he asks.

"They'll wait." I hit the turn signal again, this time to turn right toward the bank. "See you in a few." I hang up the phone, and my music pops back into the speakers. I enjoy the song on the radio, singing along, until I pull into the bank parking lot and turn off the car.

When I hop out, Henry is already standing on the sidewalk in front of the bank. He greets me with a quick peck on the cheek, partially because he hates public displays of affection at work and partially because he's obviously stressed about the issue they're having. "OK, I have no idea what's going on with the computers. I really need your help here."

"Sure." I point to the doors. "Let's walk to your office, and you can tell me what's going on." Henry walks fast when he's stressed, so he powers through the front lobby of the bank like a steam engine, chugging along without bothering to stop and wave at anyone. There are four tellers, I note, on our pass by the lobby. All of them are standing in front of computers but none of them appear to be working on them. There are customers lined up, but no one is moving. Almost everyone looks like they're in various stages of impatience. Not good, as far as signs go.

Henry swings into his office, leaving the door open, and gestures to his computer. "You know everyone connects to the terminal of the bank main system through an app when they get here. Well, that app isn't working."

"Be more specific," I say as I drop into his plush rolling chair and wiggle the mouse. It responds, so at least I know the computer isn't frozen. I'm looking at the main screen for the bank app; I've seen it before when helping with computer issues. Nothing looks obviously wrong with it.

"It's not responding. It doesn't matter what box you click in, it will ..." Henry keeps talking, but I'm not really listening. I hear the sound of his voice, but I'm investigating as he suggested. I click on the box for account number. The working icon, a small spinning circle, pops up. Then the entire window disappears as if I closed it. A smaller box pops up, this one telling me it's attempting to establish a connection with the remote desktop. That stays for about three seconds before also dropping off, leaving me staring at Henry's desktop background image.

I look up at Henry. "Have you called the main help number for the server?"

"Yes. They say everything looks fine on their end. But that can't be right, obviously. This is anything but fine. Should I call the helpline again?"

"Give me a second."

"But it takes time to get through. I'm going to call them again." He pulls his cell phone out of his pocket and starts dialing. I double click on the icon that should start a connection with the server. It pops open the same "establishing connection" box. This time it stays up and prompts with a login box.

I type Henry's name and the password he always uses. *Error: password incorrect.* "Henry, did you change your password?"

"What?" He leans down to look at what I'm doing. "Oh,

yeah. Here." He leans between me and the keyboard, typing something into the box that I can't see. I blink at him in surprise. Since when does he keep his passwords from me? Curious.

When he stands up again, the screen is back to the welcome screen for the bank interface. I click on the settings at the top; it lets me click. I take this as a good sign. I can access the settings within the device, I just can't interact with anything that would push to the server. That likely means the problem is local to this device or this office.

According to the settings, I'm communicating with the server from Location: Blackstone Hub and Device: 4A. "Henry," I say. I have to repeat his name three times before he pulls his attention from the lobby, where he is presumably watching customers become more agitated. I wait until his eyes fall on me. His cell phone is still next to his ear, but not near his mouth. I'm guessing he's on hold. "When did you add the new teller window?" I ask, gesturing toward the door. The last time I visited the bank, admittedly about two weeks ago, there were only three teller desks out there with three employees.

He looks as if the answer will be written on the air. "Um, we moved the desk in there yesterday."

"After closing?" I guess.

"Yeah. Why?"

I nod. "But you didn't get the computer up right away. When did you get that going?"

"This morning we moved it in. It was all hooked up and ready to go live right after lunch."

I nod again. I would imagine the problems started right around that same time. "Who set up the new work station?"

"I did." He comes around behind me. "Why, did I do

something wrong? I did what you showed me last time." He points to the window I have open. "Yeah, right there. I set it up like you told me, and I used that device number because it's the fourth computer." He looks at me again. "Just like you said."

"This is the device number for your computer, not the one out there."

"Oh. Is that the problem? I used the same name for both?" He shakes his head. "No, that can't be it. They're all having trouble, not just these two."

I hold up my hand, stopping him from ranting. "The duplicate name causes a host name conflict, which is housed at this location. That is going to prevent anything in this location from establishing a connection or making changes to the server."

His hand flies to his mouth. "Oh my God, I did this? You're telling me I did this?" He shakes his head. "How do we fix it?"

"It's not a big deal. Hang up the phone; we don't need them."

I click in the box for Henry's device name and change it to 5A. Henry holds the administrative account for this particular hub, meaning his access authorizes me to make this change. "Everyone out there just needs to shut down their current sessions, give it about ten seconds to take effect, and log back in." I stand up, pushing back his chair in the process. "It should all work after that."

"That's it?" He hangs up the phone where, I presume, he was still listening to hold music. "I should have called you sooner. You're an angel." He steps into his doorway. "Ladies and gentlemen, thank you for your patience. It seems we have a solution. Employees, please log out of the system for me. In just a few seconds, we'll have you log in again, and the problem should be taken care of. Everyone, please, take a bottle of water from the little fridge before you leave. I'm sorry for the wait."

He turns back to me. "Honestly, thank you. I really should've called you sooner."

"Didn't you notice the problems all started when you signed into that computer?" I ask because I can't believe no one noticed that connection.

"It didn't start when we powered it up. It didn't even start when we signed into that one. It only started later, when a different teller suddenly couldn't change anything." He rubs his hand along the back of his head where the hair is short. "I didn't even make that connection because the problem started with a different computer."

"That makes sense." I put my hand on his shoulder. "Not your fault. Simple mistake. Next time, just call me."

He smiles. "I will. I just saw that you were at the grocery store, and I figured I'd give you a little time."

I keep my smile frozen on my face even though I feel that little twinge you get only from withholding information from someone. That little rush a secret brings, like you're getting away with something. I know there's no chance anything strange or unusual popped up when he used that service, but to know he was actually looking makes me glad I had the forethought to turn them off. "Are you checking up on me?" I ask, tilting my head to the side and taking on a playful tone of voice.

Henry laughs, light and airy. The laugh of someone who sees only the humor in the situation and not anything underlyingly nefarious. "No, I just didn't want to interrupt anything important."

I lean in and kiss him, another work appropriate peck. "I love you for being considerate, even in your stress."

"I love you for rushing over here, even with groceries in the car."

I reach into the bag hanging over my shoulder and pull out the car keys. "On that note, I need to get the frozens home." I walk back out into the lobby where things have started to seem more normal. Customers have moved in line, people are being helped at the tellers, and money is being counted. Things look like they're progressing.

"We're back up, Mr. King," one employee calls. Henry waves at her with a smile.

If nothing else, this little field trip taught me one very important thing: all my careful protections really are for a purpose. Nothing I do is extraneous.

Chapter 16

BREAKING AND ENTERING isn't normally my specialty, but when William Archer leaves the window of his apartment open the next day, it feels like an invitation I can't turn down. According to the time on my dashboard, he will still be at the church for another half hour. I have time. There's also no one around the apartment complex right now.

I put on my black hat and a pair of driving gloves. Then I make my way up to the second-floor landing. From this vantage point, I notice you can see the playground of an elementary school in the distance. Why does everything in your life keep coming up children, Mr. Archer?

The windows are similar to my own, with a screen on the outside. The screen has little tabs on the sides, which help you get leverage to remove the screen. I quickly glance around to make sure no one is watching and pop the screen out. Then I scramble inside before I can change my mind. It's a little more difficult to get the screen back in from this angle, but I manage.

Only once the screen is in place do I take the

opportunity to look around. There's a kitchen off to the right, no windows because there's another unit on that side. The room I'm in appears to be a living room, with a small television and a rack of DVDs across from me. There's a couch beside me, old and ratty. There's also a small table in front of the couch, complete with a single beer bottle. Bachelor life as written by some college student studying cliche screenwriting. I wrinkle my nose. Be more original, Bill.

I move to my left through the only door I see besides the heavy front door. This door is open and leads to a bedroom. There's a full-size bed, a dresser, and a little table with a lamp and a phone charger. I also notice a bathroom on the other side of the room from where I've entered.

I honestly don't know what I'm looking for. Everything in this guy's life is like an unproved suspicion. He's a creepy older man with a penchant for beer who happens to be around children a lot. That could be nothing, or it could be my least favorite type of mark. I just need proof to help me feel like I'm making the right decision.

My first stop is the bathroom off the bedroom. The ceiling is solid, which immediately rules out the favorite hiding place of many movie bad guys. The cabinet under the sink contains nothing other than extra rolls of toilet paper, a bottle of body wash, and what might be mold.

Back in the bedroom, I take notice of the dirty carpet. Meaning no loose floorboard option either. I check the closet and find nothing hiding behind the clothes. Nothing in the dresser stands out as extraordinary. I drop to my stomach and look in my personal favorite childhood hiding spot, under the bed. Nothing but a few dust bunnies lurk there. Hard to consider that a failure when I was truly expecting bugs after the mold surprise.

I wander back out into the living room and stand for a moment in the doorway. If I were me, living here, where would I hide the things I didn't want anyone to find?

My eyes land on the fireplace. Risky option in this state where winters are actually cold enough to warrant a fireplace. But ideal for exactly that same reason—no one in their right mind would suspect you'd render a fireplace unusable in this climate.

I drop on my knees in front of the stone hearth and reach my hand up into the chimney. I run my hands along the bricks, feeling for a loose edge or something out of place. Nothing turns up.

I lean back on my heels and look around the room again. This seemed like my most solid option. I flip on my cell phone's flashlight app and shine it up into the dark throat. The light shines up into the bricks, bouncing off of the sides but disappearing into the darkness in the center. But there's nothing blocking it. Nothing hidden up there, no loose bricks.

I flop back on my knees again, turning off the light. I need a new idea. Where else would I choose to hide things if I were living here in bachelor paradise and needed some documents or items kept secret?

The oven.

The answer pops into my head almost without permission. Sure, I use my oven daily. But Bill seems to be outside of his house during mealtime most days. He spends an awful lot of time at that bar down the street. It's not outside the realm of possibility to assume he doesn't use that oven.

I make my way into the kitchen and pull open the oven

door. An empty, although dirty, oven greets me. Frustrated, I slam the oven door. The force of my slam rattles the small drawer underneath. I focus my attention there next, pulling the metal drawer open. Inside there is a small plastic box, the side of a shoebox, with a white lid. Jackpot.

I pull the white plastic lid off carefully. Part of me wants to slam my eyes shut against what could be inside this box. But I fight the urge and force myself to look at the items inside. Small squares, roughly six inches on each side, seem to fill the entire box. There's no order to them, just haphazard piles. My stomach turns when I realize what those little squares are. Polaroid pictures. I don't even want to flip them over because part of me already knows what they'll be. But I have to decide how bad this is. I have to see how far to take this.

So I turn them.

One by one, I force myself to look at the things this monster holds dear. I see faces frozen in masks of fear. I see parts of children no one but a pediatrician should have the right to see. I see tears. I see pain. I see childhood innocence shattered by one man who pretends to be godly and yet steals everything from preteen girls one click of a camera at a time.

When I hear footsteps at the front door, I don't jump in fear. Instead, I slowly stand up and slip my hand into my black boot. I wrap my hand around the handle of the Beretta .22 I had the presence of mind to bring with me today. It's the only gun I've ever owned. I normally hate guns. I've never used it for a job, only at a firing range. Yet, with all the red flags and the way this one was sitting in my gut, I think a part of me knew it would come to this. I don't have the patience to wait for Bill. I'm writing this story on the fly today.

William Archer, 47, was found dead in his apartment with what appears to be a self-inflicted gunshot wound. The bullet entered the victim under the chin and exited the top of his head. The gun, an unregistered Beretta .22, was found on the scene. The victim's fingerprints were found on the gun, and gunshot residue was found on the victim's hand and clothing.

There was also a box containing child pornography beside the victim on the couch. The box was open, and thirty-seven images were scattered around the box and the floor. The only fingerprints lifted from the box or pictures belonged to the victim.

The ME ruled this death a suicide.

In reality, it didn't take much to get William to comply. The sight of me put him on his guard, but the sight of that open box instantly put him on the defensive. He broke down, crying. I told a white lie, claiming to be a relative of my client. The fact that he instantly recognized her name made me want to shoot him right there. But that's not the best way to handle anything.

Instead, I wiped the gun down with a towel on his counter. I wiped slowly and carefully. Then I offered it to him, my hand wrapped in the towel and wrapped around the muzzle of the gun. "Take it. Do the right thing for once in your miserable life. Or we call the police and let them sort all of this out. How many years do you think you'll get for each of those pictures, Mr. Archer? How many counts are there? How many families will come forward?"

In the end, the story I told was basically what happened.

William Archer did commit suicide. It's easier when the story you have to tell is what really happened.

On my way home, I stop at the address I found for my client. I knock on the front door but don't wait for her to answer. I walk straight to her mailbox, dropping the three packets of one hundred dollar bills she gave me. Then I walk back to my car, parked across the street. When I get in the driver's seat and shut the door, I turn my head to look back at her house. She saw me, but she is standing cautiously on her front stoop. I stay in my running car, my foot nowhere near the gas pedal, until she walks slowly to the mailbox. She pulls the door open, and I watch her step back in surprise. She turns and looks at me. I give a small wave and pull away from the curb.

I'm sure she worries that it means I didn't complete the job, but I'm not worried. She'll see the news soon enough. I can't ask her to pay for this one. I hate people like Bill Archer. Besides, I didn't kill him.

He killed himself.

Chapter 17

<hr>

A SINGLE CALL came into the newest burner phone late on the following Friday night when Henry and I had just opened our second bottle of wine. Normally, I don't take calls that come in when Henry and I are spending time together, drinking. If the person wants my services badly enough, they'll call back. But Henry had just gone to the bathroom, and I answered it automatically.

The caller, a man with a deep and comforting tone of voice, followed all my rules. No attempt to use a name. Can meet me whenever I'd like; he will work around my schedule. I was just drunk enough to not want to handle it that night but just sober enough to schedule for Monday.

So after lunch on Monday, I head out wearing black yoga pants and a black sports bra. I pull on a black zip-up hooded sweatshirt and my black hat once I'm almost to the location. I park my car at a gas station and run inside to buy a bottle of water and a granola bar with cash. I finish both of them on the half-mile walk to the grocery store, where I told my Friday night caller to meet me. I toss the remnant of the snack into the trash can by the entrance to the store. But I keep walking. Past the entrance, past the regular spots, to the far end of the parking lot. There, under a tree, is a luxury SUV that almost looks familiar. Of course, it is conceivable that someone else in this neighborhood owns a so-dark-gray-it-is-almost-black Infiniti QX80. Still, my guard is up. Part of me already knows I've seen this car before.

I open the passenger side door, and panic clouds my vision. White man, mid-forties, expensive tailored suit and watch, black frames. The man from the Amtrak station is sitting in the driver's seat. He holds out his arm. "Don't leave. Just hear my proposition."

I start to push the door shut.

"I'll triple your usual fee," he says in desperation.

I freeze. "You have to stop contacting me."

"Of course. You'll never hear from me again." He gestures to the passenger seat. "Please, sit."

I shouldn't. Part of me knows that. Triple my usual fee, no matter what he thinks that is, is a lot of money. If he thinks he can offer me that, it means he has that much cash inside this car right now. What would you do for that kind of money? I'd hear someone out, that's for sure. Especially someone I can listen to in broad daylight in a public parking lot. Especially since I know about eight or nine ways I could kill him right here and basically get away with it.

I start spinning a story in my head about a man who attacked me in the grocery store, forcing me to get in his car. Yes, I can make that work for a sympathetic police officer if I have to. I could easily spin this death into self-defense, fending off my attacker.

I lower myself into the seat, which is warm from the

sunlight flooding through the windshield. The interior of the car is clean and shiny as if it was recently cleaned. Nothing else in the car seems to give me information about this client, no coffee cups or parking passes. No trash in the doors or ID card swinging from the rearview mirror. He's not wearing any specific jewelry besides the watch. He doesn't have any obvious tattoos sticking out from under his office-appropriate clothing. Basically, he's giving me nothing.

"Thank you for sitting. This is personal to me," he says. "This person has to be stopped." I try to commit his voice to memory. Would I recognize it if he called again?

Wait. I pause and break down what he just said. He just uttered my absolute favorite phrase: "personal to me." Loosely translated, that phrase normally means double the asking price. If something is personal to you, you'll pay extra for it. Combine that with his desperate offer to pay triple, and we could be talking sky's the limit kind of money. I glare at him. "One job?" I ask.

"Yes."

I combine all the facts I know so far. This client wants to take charge, meaning this is likely to be someone he thinks wronged him. He looks like he sweats cash, and he offered to triple my fee. Then he told me this is personal to him, which means even more money. This car is expensive, with leather upholstery.

I look him square in the eye when I drop the figure. "Three hundred thousand." That's enough money to replace what I just returned to the young counselor. It's enough money to let Henry and I take a big vacation. It's enough money for a lot of things.

"And we'll never have contact again," he pushes.

I flinch at the effort to keep control of this situation. I have to remain in control for this to be acceptable. "I already said that was rule number one. Whether I do this or not, you have to stop contacting me. Are we clear?"

"Crystal."

"Once you put this in motion, even God himself can not stop it from happening," I say.

The right side of his mouth twitches up at that, almost like he is fighting a smile. "Excellent." He taps the manilla envelope sitting on the console between us. "I have the picture and the name right here."

"Stop talking right now," I command, "or I will leave." I put my hand on the door handle again. I'm tempted to pull it open. So tempted that my hand actually twitches. This guy is giving me bad vibes.

"Alright, alright." He holds his hands up in surrender. "Three hundred thousand."

I watch his every movement as he slowly reaches over the center console and into the back seat. He pulls up a black canvas bag with two straps. "Set it on the console," I tell him. He complies. "Unzip it slowly." Again, he does what I ask.

Inside the bag are stacks of hundred dollar bills. My estimation skills are decent in this area, and it looks like it should be enough, assuming they are all hundreds. "You expect me to believe you have exactly the required fee inside this bag?" I ask.

He smiles. "There's actually an extra fifty thousand, but I didn't think you'd allow me to take that out of the bag."

I zip the bag shut. "Thanks for the tip."

I leave the car with the black bag, the manilla envelope, and a little less pride than I had going into the exchange.

Something about this mystery man who has contacted me before gives me a terrible feeling. I normally do not work with the same client twice. No one has ever attempted to reach out to me a second time.

Of course, technically, I haven't worked with this guy. He's attempted to contact me at least once that I know of, but it's unusual for a potential client to try again. I can bring up his voice in my mind, but I can't remember if it matches any of the calls I refused to work with. I remember a guy recently, one who was too pushy. I got rid of a disposable phone on the same day I turned it on because of a call like that. But I can't remember if the voice is the same.

Possibly because of this terrible feeling in my gut, I do something else I don't normally do. I stand in the shadows of the grocery store until I watch the client leave. I make a mental note of his license plate number: CVT771. I watch him drive out of the lot, down the street, and out of sight. Then I count to fifty before I move again. No sirens fill the air; no police come streaming in to bust me for agreeing to a hit on someone.

I shove the manilla envelope into the back of my yoga pants and pull my sweatshirt down over it. The black bag itself is conspicuous enough; I don't also need an envelope. I try to look normal while walking back with it, my eyes on guard for police vehicles or almost black luxury SUVs.

I tell myself that I have to face the inevitable likelihood that the picture inside this envelope is someone important with high security. Perhaps a politician or a local news personality. This kind of money isn't thrown around for the average Jane

Doe. What will I do when I open it and see that?

I decide I'll turn to the police at that point. I have the license plate number of the man who gave me the cash. I'll tell them he gave me two hundred and fifty thousand, keeping the rest as a sort of finders fee. I'll promise to give them everything I know only for immunity. Then, I can leave town after this is all done. I'm not sure how I'll convince Henry to leave town, but I'm sure I can come up with something.

Half a block away, I realize I wouldn't do that. I wouldn't waltz into a police department and say, "I offered to kill someone for money, but I can't kill this person. Here's everything you need to suddenly question me about previous hits." That would be a colossal mistake. That would open up the entire police department into my past. I'll have to come up with something else.

What if I found a way to do it? I can find the client and ask for even more once I see the high-profile picture. I could retire. Henry and I could kick back and enjoy the luxury life for a few years. We can drink wine and read books. We can binge-watch TV shows and nap.

I shake my head. I'm not cut out for that kind of future. I would miss death, I think. That sounds bad, but at least I know myself well enough to know that. But, as an idea, asking for money does have promise. A little more padding is reasonable if this really is personal to him. If the person in that envelope is someone big, someone with security, it just makes sense.

I could do it, I'm sure. I could find a way to make whatever this is happen. I can do anything. I am in control. I can make this work in my favor no matter who is in that envelope—I'm sure of it.

Chapter 18

THE LAST QUARTER mile of my walk goes quickly. I keep my brain occupied with details of what steps I need to take next. Build a file on the client, of course. If anyone is a potential candidate for blackmailing in the future, it's this asshole who insisted on breaking all of my rules. In fact, I decide that I will do that research no matter who is in the envelope. The desire to know everything about this shady rich man drives my feet to move even faster.

I throw the black bag in the trunk of my car and bring the manilla envelope with me into the cab, tossing it on the passenger seat beside me. When I turn on the car, the radio pops on, blaring something loud that sounds like screaming. I wrench the knob to the left, quieting the singer. Clearly, I'm a different person right now than I was when I got out of the car.

I start the car and pull out into traffic. I follow all the traffic laws, despite my brain being hung up on research and what could be inside that envelope. There's no way it's just a normal client, so I'm preparing myself. You don't offer to triple someone's fee for a normal hit. I glance over at the envelope, the color popping against the black seat of my car. It has to be someone secure, someone big, or someone important. Someone that will take me a lot of time and energy to get to. It's obvious this client doesn't think this will be easy. Is that because he underestimates me? I glance at the envelope again. Am I capable of pulling off whatever this is?

I come to a stop at the red light ahead and internally battle with myself about opening it here. I really shouldn't. I should wait until I'm home and there's no risk of some cell phone camera from a nearby car or a traffic camera picking up a video of me opening this envelope and finding whatever I'm about to find. I'm being paranoid, I know. But what if that picture is the head of a major news network or the president of a major corporation? That would be a high-profile case, and high-profile means high scrutiny. I can't afford any mistakes this time around. I have to do everything by the book, and that includes opening this envelope in my own home where I control the footage.

Still, my hand moves over to the seat, caressing the envelope as if checking to make sure it is still there. With my eyes transfixed on the red light, I let my fingers dance over the flap at the back of the envelope. It's sealed. Not only with the little metal tab, which is typically used to secure these, but completely sealed. Someone took the time to lick the flaps and close the metal fastener. That confirms my suspicion that this is someone important. Why go through all that trouble if no one would know the person in the envelope anyway? It also means if I pull a few strings and call in a few favors, I may have access to this asshole's DNA.

The light turns green, and I roll through the intersection with the other cars. I have to get my mind to focus. I have to act like things are normal. So I hit the talk button on my steering wheel. The robotic voice of the car's Bluetooth system plays through the stereo. "Please say a command."

"Call Henry," I say.

"Calling Henry." The center console changes to show Henry's name, and the sound of ringing fills the car.

It rings twice before Henry's voice comes through. "Hello, beautiful. How are you today?"

"Stressed," I answer honestly. "Work is giving me a major headache. I needed a break. How are things there?"

"Nothing unusual here. It's actually been a pretty slow day. I have a mortgage client coming in to sign paperwork around four, but I should still be out on time." Henry is the branch manager of a small bank in town. His job, aside from being the final word on loans, is mostly about keeping other people doing their job. For that, he makes a salary better than those of all the people really doing the hard work. At least, that's how he explains it. "Would you like to go out to dinner, maybe buy an expensive bottle of something after your hard day?"

I sigh. "I could be talked into that." Traffic in front of me slows, brake lights flashing into my car. I follow suit, giving myself plenty of room in case the lane to my right opens up before this one does. "That actually sounds like a brilliant plan. Meet me at home and we'll ride together?"

"Of course," Henry says. "Are you home now?"

I consider lying for a heartbeat. But despite the whopper about what I really do for a living, we don't actually lie to each other. I mean, I don't lie to him. I certainly hope he doesn't lie to me. "No, I had to swing by and pick something up from a client," I explain. "He was completely rude, too. Wanted to control everything and act like he was in charge."

Henry laughs. "Oh, you hate that."

"I do." But the sound of his laughter makes me smile and, honestly, right this second, I feel a little better. Traffic in front of me starts moving again, and I join them. We're moving slowly, barely rolling. "Traffic is awful tonight," I tell him. "What time did you say you were heading home in this mess?"

I look down at the console. Normally, he'd have about an hour left. "Same time," he says. "You think I should take another route home? Is something blocking the road?"

I lean my body to the side, trying to see around the car in front of me. "I can't tell," I say. "I'll let you know if I see an accident or something when I get closer. But you have an hour before you're rolling through this area, so I'm sure it will be alright. An hour is plenty of time to clear up whatever this is."

"Great," Henry says. "I'll see you at home. I'll even call a few places and score us some dinner reservations. Try not to scream at any bossy clients before I can be there to witness everything."

This time, it's my laughter ringing through the car, and it breaks up the last of the anger in my chest. "Thanks, honey. Talk soon. I love you."

"Love you, too."

I punch the button for the red disconnect function in the car. I swear I only look down for a millisecond, but when I look back up, the brake lights of the car in front of me are too close. I slam my foot back down on the break. Luckily, we had barely gotten up to a roll, so the car stops pretty quickly.

But the momentum knocks the envelope onto the floor. I stare at it down there on the floorboards and feel the anger rushing back. Suddenly, I can't be patient. I have to know what picture is in that envelope. I have to know if this is someone important.

I keep my foot pressed on the brake pedal and reach over. My fingertips find the envelope easily, and I bring it back up to the seat. I check the traffic, which has moved about ten feet. I roll up behind the car in front of me and come to another stop.

Then I pull the envelope into my lap.

I watch the traffic, looking for anyone with a camera. Seeing no one, I slip my finger under the seal, breaking the connection between the flap and the envelope. Still, traffic stands still. It's as if fate has decided I have time for this right now.

I reach my hand inside, my eyes still on the car in front of me. My fingers graze what feels like two pieces of paper. I pinch my first two fingers around them and slowly tug them toward the flap. I keep telling myself I'll stop if traffic moves, stop if I hear sirens, stop if my phone rings.

None of that happens.

The two pieces of paper come free of the flap. I can see them out of the bottom of my eye, enough to see color, which tells me they are not upside down. I make sure the one I assume is a picture is on top. Then I flick my eyes down to it.

My brain registers an image but doesn't have time to process before my eyes are back on the bumper of the car in front of me.

Then, like a computer that has finally finished buffering, my brain catches up. But what my brain is telling me can't be right.

I pull my eyes back down to the image, really looking at it.

I pull it closer to my face and examine the blonde hair sticking out of the black hat. I look at the jeans from Old Navy, the black Nike running shoes, the black t-shirt and black hooded sweatshirt. I analyze every detail, trying to find something that doesn't match what I already know I'll see. Anything at all that looks out of place.

All I need is one detail that doesn't make this a picture of me outside of my own house.

I slip the photo back into the envelope and get confirmation that I'm not going to find those details. Staring me right in the face in blocky handwriting using all capital letters is the name of the mark.

My own name. Regina King.

Chapter 19

<hr>

"REGINA," HENRY'S VOICE cuts through my mental fog. He's irritated. I can tell by the harder R in my name and the deeper tone of his voice.

I shake my head and sigh. "I'm sorry. I told you it was a shitty day. What were we talking about?" I take a bite of my scallops to show that I'm back to our dinner.

"Is there anything I can do?" he asks, taking a drink of his red wine. "I hate seeing you so upset. I know you said you can't tell me about the job, but maybe you can give me a hypothetical."

Hypothetically a guy just tried to tell me to kill myself for three hundred and fifty thousand dollars, dear. No, I can't say that. I shake my head. "It's hard to break down like that." Henry frowns. I take a deep breath; I have to try. I have to give him something. He's trying to be supportive. "Someone asked me to do something I absolutely cannot do. So either they're trying to pull some kind of prank, they're trying to get me to admit that I cannot do it, or they seriously expect me to attempt this impossible task."

Henry frowns. Then he takes a bite of his salmon and

chews it very slowly. Finally, after swallowing, he takes a deep breath. "I thought doing impossible things just to prove they could be done was basically your job description."

Right. In the day job where I spend my time hacking into impossible-to-hack systems, that would be a pretty accurate description. "Yes, well. This can't be done."

"So you can't get access, but someone wants you to?"

"Something like that."

Henry's blue eyes meet mine directly, and something keeps me frozen there, unable to look away. I think it's his intensity, suddenly turned up all the way. "Is this something illegal they're asking you to do?" he asks.

My heartbeat doubles. "Possibly," I answer, my voice a whisper.

Henry pinches his lips together and shakes his head. "Shit," he breathes. "That sucks. I'm sorry they're putting you through that." He reaches out and takes my hand where it's sitting on the top of the table. He rubs his thumb over the back of my hand. "You don't just want to tell them to fuck off?"

I smile at the phrasing. "I'd love to, but I already got paid."

He throws his head back and breathes out in frustration. "So what are the options? Besides doing it, which seems ridiculous."

I flip my hand around and squeeze his fingers. "Honestly, I don't know yet. I just heard about this today. I don't think I've fully wrapped my head around it. Let me do a little research, and I'm sure I can figure something out."

Henry smiles, which tells me that I successfully pitched my voice into a more pleasing octave. He thinks I'm relaxing.

I take a big swig of my wine and another bite of scallop. "I'm going to figure out how to make this work."

He drops my hand and returns his to his lap. "Good. Maybe you can figure out a subtle, work-appropriate way to tell them to fuck off."

"I hope so."

We finish our main courses in a more comfortable sort of quiet. Then the waitress returns. "Can I interest you in dessert?" she asks. I notice the little rectangular dessert menu is already tucked into her apron. We come here often, and dessert is one thing we normally indulge in when we go out to eat.

But I'd like to go home and start on that research. I need to find out who this guy in the expensive SUV with pictures of me outside my home really is. I need to know everything about him. I frown at Henry. "I think I want to pass tonight if that's alright with you."

Something flashes in his eyes, but it's gone before I can figure out what it might have been. Then he's smiling at the waitress. "We'll just take the check this time, but thank you."

She pulls the check from behind the dessert menu and hands it over. "No problem. You folks have a nice evening."

Henry drops cash into the black folder and closes it. I don't ask if he left a tip because I have known Henry long enough to know he did, and likely a generous one. Instead, I stand up and head toward the front door. My husband's hand falls warm and supportive on my lower back, letting me know he is behind me.

At the car, I drop into the passenger seat, content to let Henry control our ride home while I attempt to relax a little more. He starts the car and pulls out onto the road. "Do you have any enemies that you know of?" I ask.

Henry turns toward me, his eyebrows pulled together skeptically. "What?"

"Enemies. Like someone who wants to see you or someone you love harmed." It's something I've been wondering about myself. But, obviously, that list has the potential to be a lot longer. I'm always careful with my hits. There are no records that it was me, and the marks are always people who generally the world is better without. But still, not everyone will think that.

Take Christina Montenegro, for example. I know there's a sister who lives in Texas. It's conceivable that the sister would think Christina was a generally good person. Maybe she had no idea what her sister was doing with her life. It's possible someone like that would blame me. I could go on about how ridiculous that is, especially since I was just carrying out what her husband would have found a way to do eventually. But I won't. Instead, I want to focus on eliminating the more far-fetched possibility that this person has connections to my Henry.

"None," he answers.

"Think harder," I admonish. "I just want to be sure."

He sighs. "Regina, there's no one who hates me enough to ask you to do some illegal job hacking something you shouldn't."

His thumbs start tapping on the steering wheel. I notice they're on the downbeats for the song playing softly in the background. For some people, like me, this is a sign we're enjoying our drive and the music. For my husband, this is his attempt to focus. He was a drummer in high school. Listening to the beat of the music helps his mind narrow down onto one task;

it's automatic.

"I was just making sure," I say. I lay my hand on his arm. "Sorry. I'm just stressed about this whole thing."

"It'll work out," he says. "You'll do some looking into it, and you'll find a solution. You're brilliant." He flashes a quick smile at me before putting his eyes back on the road. "I wouldn't want to be the one who presented this challenge to you. They're going to regret it for sure."

At home, I tell Henry I want to do some research and take my laptop out into the sunroom. He opens a bottle of wine, this one white, and brings me a glass. I choose the seat on the little outdoor style couch that points my screen at the windows, instead of toward the center of the room where Henry might see what I'm working on. The sunroom looks out over our back yard and woods, so it's highly unlikely anyone would be nearby to look in the window. Add to that the fact that our backyard slopes downward, meaning our sunroom is raised up a level, and it becomes impossible to believe someone lurking about would be able to see what I'm working on. Even still, I begin by going through the motions of turning up the security and firewalls on this device. Only when I'm convinced that I'm working securely do I start my digging.

Normally, when I do my research, I start with the mark. That will often lead to a connection, allowing me to recognize the face of the client. Obviously in this case, that's not going to work. So, instead, I'm going to have to dig with the license plate number.

Now, I don't work for law enforcement and, unlike all the movies would have you believe, I can't just call up some dirty cop on my payroll and ask them to run the license plate. Instead,

I turn to the internet. There are a shocking number of sources that will allow you to put in license plate numbers and return a name and a state. Really, a name is all I need. I type in the license plate number I memorized at the meeting and wait for the results to load.

Stewart Houston.

It's one of three possible names returned on the list, but it's the only one that sounds even remotely familiar. The problem is, I can't remember why I know that name.

I pop open my own files and run a search for that name. Maybe this is someone I've worked with before? Nothing comes up.

I run a search online for the name. He's forty-five, and he works downtown for a local internet security company. Perhaps that's how I know him. Maybe he hired me in my day job to try and break into one of his servers?

I open a non-secure browser and my personal, clean files. I run a search for his last name. Nothing comes up.

I close everything down and blow off the history of the search. For now, I have everything I need for my next move. I'm going to break one of my own rules.

Tomorrow, I'm paying Stewart Houston a visit at work.

Chapter 20

THE NEXT MORNING, I join Henry in the shower before he leaves for work. He's shocked when I first climb in, but it doesn't take him long to realize what is going on and relax. Shower sex is something I have a strong appreciation for, mostly because it's incredibly clean. I hope this small act shows Henry I'm sorry for ruining our dinner and I'm feeling much more confident going into today. I have a plan, and that's all that I need.

After the shower, I dress in jeans and a black button-up shirt. I keep my hair loose. Then I put on black boots with a tall heel. It won't be enough to give me a height advantage over Stewart, but never underestimate the intimidating power of a woman in heels. I think it reminds men that we can take anything. After all, we torture ourselves with footwear just to look good.

The office building I found the address for is downtown. I absolutely hate downtown because the streets all go one way, we have annoying parking rules, and there is a shocking number of vehicles there. But I bring an extra dose of patience and head out.

Thanks to a quick search on my phone, I find a parking garage close to the building that has public parking for five dollars. I take my little ticket, park, and put the ticket on the dashboard. I'm not going to bother bringing it in to get it validated. Stewart and I have plenty to talk about without worrying about the five-dollar parking fee.

I grab the bag full of cash, the exact one he handed me, from the backseat and lock the car on my way out of the garage. The noise of the alarm echoes through the garage. So does the sound of my heels clicking on the concrete. I pause, listening for more footsteps. Normally, I don't worry about being followed, but this interaction is anything but ordinary so it can't hurt to be cautious.

Hearing nothing out of the ordinary, I hurry along. I can see the building, which I found a picture of online, in the distance. The lobby of the building has a tall ceiling and a few chairs for waiting. There's a security guard in a blue shirt at the front counter. He nods at me when I open the large front door. "Can I help you?" he asks. No smile, just matter-of-fact.

"I have an appointment with Stewart Houston from Innovative IT Solutions."

"Name?"

"Regina King." No point in keeping my identity a secret; clearly, he already knows who I am.

"One second." He picks up a phone on his left and hits a single button, never taking his eyes off me. "Mr. Houston, I have a Regina King for her meeting." There's a pause. I try to figure out what that pause might mean. Did Stewart go with option number one—admit that we have no meeting, or did he go with option number two—take the meeting because he already expected me to question this? "Thank you." The security guard hangs up the phone and hands me a plastic badge with the word "Visitor" in black block letters. "Take the elevator up to the eleventh floor. Someone will meet you there."

"Thank you." I pin the badge on my chest and follow his instructions.

When the elevator doors open, a young girl with straight black hair and a vividly pink dress is standing in front of them. "Ms. King?" she greets.

"That's me." I point to the visitor badge.

"Right this way."

I follow the girl into a back office with an entire wall of glass windows. There's a single table in here with six chairs around it. "You can sit anywhere you'd like," she says. "Mr. Houston will be with you shortly."

I don't sit—another power move. Instead, I stand between the table and the window and look out over the city. It's beautiful from up here. High enough to not see all the traffic and the people milling around down there. Eleven floors up gives me a decent vantage point to see the ocean in the distance. I live about an hour from here, more inland. I see the ocean sometimes but not frequently. It's beautiful from here.

I'm not so engrossed in the view that I miss the sound of the door opening behind me. I check the reflection in the glass. I can't make out the face, but the height, build, and suit are right for my client. I turn quickly on my heel and come face to face with the man who tried to pay me to kill myself.

I drop the canvas bag on the table, enjoying the loud echo that bounces off the windows. "Nice try, Stewart, but we both know this little joke has gone far enough." I lean back a little and cross my arms in front of my chest. The image I'm going for is slightly amused but very dangerous.

Stewart pulls the chair closest to him out away from the table and sits. Now the table and the bag full of hundred dollar bills are between us. He rests his arms on the sides of the chair and stares at me without speaking. It rattles me, but I try to hide it. Stewart was too eager on the phone, and he came across as almost comically cocky when we met. This version of him is the man that was underneath all that.

This man is used to being in control, and he thinks he has that in this meeting.

My chest aches for this situation I've pulled myself into. Taking that meeting with him was a huge mistake. For the first time in a long time, I'm scared.

I swallow that fear and dig deep for my anger. I seize control of it and will it to show on my face. Then, I drop my hands to my sides. "Obviously, we are not going to be working together—" I launch into what I expect to be a quick but decisive speech.

Stewart cuts me off. "Sit, Regina."

I raise one eyebrow and glare at him. He shakes his head. "Fine, stay standing. I don't really care. But I'm planning on telling you a story, and I don't expect to rush the main point, so listen carefully." He leans forward in his chair, resting his elbows on his knees. "You remind me of my sister, you know. She was hard-headed and conniving." He smiles. "I mean that as a compliment. She never met someone she couldn't manipulate into doing something for her. She had these masks she would wear with different people; she was powerful at work, she was weak for a man, she was sweet at church. Then one day, my sister left her car running inside her garage with the door closed. Can you imagine what happened next?"

"She died?" I ask. He's using the past tense; that's what really tells me. Having the garage door down and a car running would take a while to kill you unless you were incapacitated or immunocompromised. But the past tense means it worked. It's not really an efficient measure of suicide, so most often, it is seen as an accident.

"She certainly did. The police investigator ruled her death was an accident. An unfortunate accident." He allows a moment of silence, which I do not interrupt, for the passing of his sister. I'm wondering where this is all going.

Stewart leans back, lacing his fingers in front of his stomach. "I didn't believe that ruling. My sister was not the type to be forgetful like that. She was not suicidal. Plus, my research tells me it should have taken a minimum of two full minutes before the garage was full of carbon monoxide. It's likely she would've had to sit in that car with it running for about five minutes before she would pass out and the carbon monoxide could finish the job." He shakes his head. "She wouldn't do that. Not by accident."

"So, what's your working theory, Stewart?" Alarm bells are starting to go off in my head. I want to ask when she died, where she lived, and what her name was. I want to know how this connects to me, even as gray ribbons that might be connections are starting to show themselves in my dread.

"I told you to sit; I'm not going to rush this. A good story takes time, Regina." He points to the chair across from him. I wait for a full breath cycle, debating. Finally, I pull the chair towards me and drop into it. Neither of us is close to the table. Really, someone could get up and run laps around the table without hitting either of us. I have plenty of time to react if Stewart starts moving.

"I hired a private investigator to look into my sister's death. He found that she had recently begun dating a man. Bank records showed that the man had made some rather large deposits into my sister's account. When I received the contents of my sister's house, I found some jewelry, expensive jewelry, that I didn't know the origins of. The PI was able to trace the purchases back to the store and got a description of a man who looked like the boyfriend. That tells us he was buying her expensive jewelry and giving her money. I told you, she can be manipulative. Would you like to guess what I think happened next?"

My palms are sweating a little. He seems to be dancing too close to a story I've heard. The girl dumps the boy, and he thinks he's been swindled. Maybe there's evidence she'd done this to other men, other sets of jewelry, other expensive purchases. Maybe the house with the garage and the car she used aren't even ones she paid for herself. Maybe the boyfriend snaps and hires someone to do his dirty work for him. "Why don't you just tell me?" I say.

"Well, I'd love to fill in all those details for you with hard facts. But it turns out the boyfriend overdosed on drugs about two days after my sister was declared dead. I was able to convince the landlord to let me go through his belongings before they were donated to a local shelter. That's where I found the most interesting things."

He leans forward again. "Shoot, I think I've messed up the most important part of this story. I never told you their names, did I?" He stares into my eyes, meaning he's looking for my reaction. I try to force myself to stay calm. Keep a straight face. "My sister was Angelica Ripple, and her boyfriend was Fred Scott."

Fuck. I slip my tongue between my teeth and bite it to keep the expressions off my face. Fred Scott was a client. He received package C—I blackmailed him for another ten thousand dollars after the death of Angelica. His death was not on me. Well, I suppose it could've been the blackmail that drove him to an excessive amount of drugs. But he was a drug user all along.

Here I was, hoping I had no connection to Stewart, and it looks like he's found me. He's found proof of what I do for a living. Alarm bells are going off all around my head, clouding my vision. This is bad.

I clear my throat before speaking, to attempt to keep my voice even. "What happens next?" I ask.

"What a wonderful question, Regina. I could take the information I found and a picture of you meeting with Fred to the police. I could tell them I followed you to a meeting. I can tell them that I have a tape of our meeting. But you're careful, aren't you, Regina? You have never come right out and said what you do for people. So my evidence would probably not be enough for you to get the death penalty, which is what you deserve.

"But it would become something public. Something that rips apart your careful little life. Something Henry King finds out about." He smiles at me, and the hatred behind that look makes me want to melt into the floor. "So this goes one of two ways, Regina. Either you take that money"—he gestures to the black bag still between us on the table—"and your husband can keep it when you die, or you refuse to play, and I take everything

I have to the police and let them sort it out."

Obviously, I hate both of those options. I hate them both so much that my vision is going black around the edges just trying to process them. I have to find a way out of this. I have to find a magic third option, one that gets Stewart Houston off my back. To do that, I need more time. There's only one option he's put on the table here that gives me more time.

I stand up and wrap my hand around the handles of the bag. "Fuck you," I whisper.

"Same to you, sweetheart."

Chapter 21

I HOLD IT together until I drop into my car. Then I slam my hand into my steering wheel repeatedly. It's cliche, it's beneath me, but I do it. I even holler a little into the empty darkness. I hate this. I hate this man, and I hate that he's so close to what I do for a living. I hate this situation. This is everything I have never let myself be afraid of. This is my absolute worst nightmare.

Ok, I have to pull it together here. I have to find other options besides the two he has given me. There's the obvious, I could flip the hit. It's not something normally done, obviously. Basically, the idea there is that you take out the client who has paid for the hit instead of the mark themselves. The problem with this scenario is that you have to be able to erase all signs of interaction between you and the client. In this case, there are a lot of those.

First, the records of the calls to the burner, which could raise suspicion even if they cannot connect the calls to me. I'm not even sure how many times Stewart called me. Then there's the evidence he says he has, which I have no idea how to locate. I could start by checking to see if there's a safety deposit box registered in his name, which is the most common place to store things like that. But gaining access to those is practically impossible. Just another thing the movies get wrong. Then I have to consider anything Stewart may have in his possession but chose not to mention in his villain monologue. Examples of this would likely include an original of the picture he included in the envelope.

For all those reasons, flipping the hit in this scenario is definitely problematic. With a little digging, it may actually prove to be impossible.

I notice my blood pressure is coming back down, my heartbeat returning to a normal rhythm and intensity. Whether from my formulation of a plan, even a problematic one, or from the outburst in the car, I'm not sure. But I'm glad it's lowering.

I could just sever contact. I have the money here in the car, but I could string him out indefinitely and never actually do it. Of course, I have to wonder how long he'll wait. Will he go to the police after a week? After a month?

Oh, shit. What if he hires someone else?

I imagine I'm not the only game in town. It's not like we have meetings or anything, but I'm sure you could find someone else willing to make three hundred thousand dollars for one day of work.

Heck, there's probably even bottom feeders out there who would take the job just on the promise that there's a black duffle bag somewhere in my house loaded with hundred-dollar bills. He doesn't even have to tell someone directly; he can just drop that hint at the right crack house, and Henry and I are both in danger.

Henry—that's my real problem here. Stewart had his name. He brought Henry into his little discussion flippantly, like you'd mention you left a light on in the living room. That means Henry is in serious danger. If I try to run from this hit, Stewart may just order one on Henry with someone else. I have to protect Henry.

What if I just let this all come out? I roll my neck around, letting the pain from the kinks I've developed resonate through my muscles. What if I tell Stewart, as Henry put it, to fuck off? I let him take what he has to the police. I force him into the box of explaining everything. What happens then?

It's likely he doesn't really have any proof. If he did, he would've skipped this whole order-a-hit game and just gone to the police, right? Isn't that what normal people do when they're confronted with proof of a crime?

Henry is the one thing preventing me from doing that. I can't let Henry be that guy on the news who is constantly berated with questions about who his wife really was. *Are you telling us you didn't really know? How did she keep this a secret from you? What else was she hiding?* Questions like that will force Henry to wonder what else I may have lied about. He will feel like everything in our history is a lie. I can't do that to him.

Maybe I should call the police. I'm basically being blackmailed here. I shake my head. Obviously, that's a terrible idea. That would require me explaining my connection to Stewart, which is basically that I set the death of his sister in motion. I can't even pin it on the guy who ordered the hit in that case because he died of a drug overdose. Again, that one was not my fault. But once I admit I may have played a role in Angela's death, any cop worth their shield would be suspicious. Do I have any way to concretely prove I didn't hand him the drugs that killed him? I have no idea.

I could run. That's always an option when you are in my line of work. I have bags packed around my house at all times in case of an emergency. But if I'm being honest, in each hiding spot, there is a bag for me and a bag for Henry. In all my scenarios where our lives are in danger and we have to run, I never imagine doing it alone. Henry is my rock. What could I possibly tell Henry that would justify running? He would never understand.

I could just do it, I realize. I'm sure I could find a drug I could overdose on that would kill me without being messy for Henry to clean up. I can find a way to end my own life and leave my husband with the three hundred thousand dollars. Maybe I can write him some kind of letter, just for him. I can explain that I really do love him, but I kept this one secret. I can point him to the other bank accounts; he can have it all. I don't even know exactly how much money it is, but it's a lot. Enough that he would never have to worry again.

Suddenly, I feel cold. Was I really just sitting in my car in a dark parking garage contemplating killing myself so that Stewart fucking Houston would win?

I thrust the keys into the ignition and yank them clockwise to turn on the car. He will not win. I will come up with a way to get out of this.

Chapter 22

I DO A double take when my garage door rolls up in response to the button pushed in my car because Henry's car is in the garage. I shake off the surprise and park my car behind his in the driveway. Then I try to swallow all of my anger and fear at the situation with Stewart until a time when I can properly deal with it, turn off the ignition of my car, grab my purse, and open the car door.

The door onto the front deck from the house opens, and Henry is standing there, in jeans and a tee shirt, with a huge smile and a cup of something sending steam up into the air. "Hi," I say, my voice holding the unasked question.

"Hey there. It was a pretty quiet day around the bank, so I decided to leave Mikey in charge and come check on my beautiful wife and her strange work situation that may or may not involve something illegal." He holds out the mug in my direction. "Coffee?"

I can't let him walk all the way up to the car, I realize. The black bag full of cash is directly behind the center console, easily visible from the right angle. I push myself out of the car, slam the door, and walk toward him. "Coffee sounds amazing." I take a sip. "I actually just came from a meeting with them. Let's have some lunch; I'll tell you all about it."

Henry turns and heads back into the house. My mental wheels are spinning as I follow him. How do I tell him about what is happening but make it sound like it's in relation to an IT job? I don't want to outright lie to him, but I also don't want to drag him into all of this. I have to be smart.

"Leftover chicken and rice?" Henry asks.

"What?"

He stops, turns around. "For lunch. Do you want leftover chicken and rice?"

Right. Lunch. "That sounds perfect."

He smiles. "Great, I'll just heat it up. You take off your shoes and get comfortable."

I head up to the bedroom and drop onto the bed to take off my boots. My fingers are practically aching to go downstairs and start researching Stewart. I'd like to dig into him and see what I can find. Maybe I'll find myself a magic option that solves everything. Wouldn't that be nice?

No. I owe Henry a nice lunch and some conversation. I put my shoes on the shelf they belong on and pad my way back down to the dining room. Henry has heated the leftovers in the microwave and put them on plates he is now carrying to the dining room table. "Is coffee fine, or do you want something else to drink?"

I tip the mug up and take a sip of the lightly vanilla-flavored dark roast. "Coffee is perfect," I answer.

He sits behind one plate and gestures to the other. "Lunch is served." I take my seat and get exactly one bite in my mouth before he prompts, "So tell me about this meeting."

I swallow. "It didn't go well." I take another bite, chew, swallow. "Don't judge me too harshly for this. It turns out the illegal thing they're asking me to do is something I have done in the past."

Henry sucks in a breath.

"Worse, they have proof that I've done it. At least, they say they do."

"So your options are do this illegal thing again, or they turn over the proof that you've done it for a competitor?" he asks.

I shrug. Basically, that's what is happening.

"Shit," Henry says. He takes another bite of his food, chewing slowly as if contemplating. "What do you want to do?" he asks. Then he holds up a hand. "Wait, actually, I have a different question I want to ask first. How bad is this thing they're asking you to do? I mean, I know you said 'illegal,' but are we talking like jaywalking level illegal or like bombing a building level illegal?"

Good question, Henry. Perhaps not one I'm qualified to answer. After all, to someone like Henry (or you, dear reader), taking the life of someone would probably be on the top half of that scale, I would imagine. For me, it's solidly in the middle in most cases. In some cases, it's actually lower.

I sigh. "It would have serious repercussions. If I were caught and they could prove I had done it, it would mean jail time."

"Shit." He's liking that word today. "Alright, now the other question. What do you want to do? What is your gut telling you?"

My fork has been poised over my plate for a few seconds.

The food is likely returning to its lukewarm state. I force myself to lower the utensil and take a bite. I take my time chewing and swallowing. "I'm still waiting for some magic solution where everyone wins to fall from the sky, honestly." He smiles like I'm joking. I'm not. "I hate both of their solutions. I hate that I'm even in this situation. I need to find a way out that they haven't thought of yet."

He nods. "How can I help?"

"You're doing it. Let me talk about it when I need to. Remind me to eat. Love me no matter what happens." I smile at him. "Thank you for not judging me too harshly when I said I'd already done this illegal thing."

"You realize we'll have to come back to that someday, right?" His eyes narrow. "I'm not pushing it right now, but someday, I'm going to want to know what that was."

"Alright." Not now. I need time to figure out what lie I'm going to tell him.

"Finish your lunch," Henry says. "Then you can work for a bit while I go to the gym. Maybe we can get in a different kind of workout later." He winks at me in case I have trouble figuring out what he is implying.

I laugh. "Perfect."

When our plates are empty, I take them to the kitchen and wash them up. Then I leave them in the strainer to dry and make my way to the computer. Henry pokes his head in a little while later. I notice he's changed into his gym clothes. "I'm off to the gym. Try to relax. You'll find a solution." He kisses me and disappears toward the garage.

I go through the security motions before starting my research. Then I pull up my files on Angela Ripple. It's exactly like I remember it and, disgustingly, exactly like Stewart said. Angela reads like a serial golddigger if such a thing exists. The house she lived in was in the name of a guy she had dated for about two years back in her twenties. The car she drove was a purchase by another ex-boyfriend, who paid cash. Jewelry, clothes, shoes, and more all seemed to be bought and paid for by various gentlemen. As far as I could tell, Angela Ripple didn't work. But her lavish lifestyle was nevertheless paid for.

I flagged these two as option C for the same reasons I already recalled. Fred Scott, the client, was a drug user with a temper. Although I felt bad for him that Angela had picked him as a victim, I was glad to see his money flowing to her instead of into his veins. I picked up where she left off shortly after she died. From my notes, I see that I really only took one future payment of only five thousand dollars. I have a copy of the picture I used, which looks like Fred's car with two people inside but isn't really us.

If this is the picture Stewart has, he's got absolutely nothing. This could be anyone.

Of course, it did come from my secure email account. I'll have to close that, but obviously, that's not a problem. Of course, Stewart also said he has followed me and even that he has a recording of our conversations. There may not be enough to convict me based on this picture, but who knows what else he has. Plus, all of that added to what I've told Henry would be enough to convince my husband of what I do for a living if Stewart decided to go that route. Honestly, isn't that just as bad?

I'm being ridiculous. I need to avoid jail first. What would the police need? Could Stewart have any proof from the actual hit? No, that's ludicrous. Angela ordered a coffee before coming home that afternoon. I waited until she went into the bathroom, leaving her coffee on a little table she had been sitting at with her laptop. I dropped a few diphenhydramine tablets into the cup—three if I remember correctly. Then I simply followed her back to her house. She sipped on that coffee the entire way there, draining the cup before she got home. It made her tired, exhausted, error-ridden. Then, when she closed the garage door, I slipped into the house through a back window.

Angela Ripple did remember to turn her car off, as it turns out. But she did also fall asleep in the car. In the time it took me to park, wait for about five minutes to see if anything happened, walk around back, and get in the back window, she had fallen asleep with her head on the headrest and the car door open. I used my gloved hand to reach around her and turn the car back on before exiting exactly the same way I came in.

Lots of things could have gone wrong, I suppose. Someone could have seen me on her property. There didn't appear to be any neighbors with security cameras, but I could have missed one and been caught on camera. It's possible. Traces of the medication wouldn't be something you test for in a normal screen. It's too common, featured in countless over-the-counter medications. Even if someone did notice remnants of it in her coffee cup, no one would question her taking it herself for allergies. Besides, the fact that it's common means it would be impossible to trace it back to me and my purchase of the drug.

Then there's the coffee shop. That was my biggest risk. Public place, customers and employees in the store. It's not only possible but actually probable that someone saw me slip something in her drink. At the time, I assumed no one saw because no one alerted her. But perhaps they didn't remember until later. Perhaps they contacted Stewart? It's a stretch. Again, normal people who find evidence of a crime call the police. They don't call rich brothers of victims in deaths ruled accidental. I'm stretching here. No, that job was done clean, and it was done right. The answer isn't in that hit.

Time to look into Stewart a little more.

He is forty-five years old, and he has lived in Massachusetts his entire life. He was born in Framingham and now resides in Cambridge. I sigh. Cambridge means big money. There's no way this lack of three hundred thousand dollars is hurting his bank account. He has never been married, has zero children to feed and clothe, has his picture in an investor's magazine, which means he heavily invests money in the stock market, and owns at least two properties that I can find. This guy is not hurting for money at all. In fact, I'd be willing to bet he could afford to pay this kind of money again to someone else to finish the job if I'm unwilling. Not good.

Images of his primary residence online show me a large white and light blue house with a double porch and a few privacy trees. It looks like every suburban television show ever shot, honestly. It's beautiful, and on television, it would project the perfect family house. In reality, the massive square footage and back lawn on this property help to explain why, according to one website, the last sale price of this house was over three million dollars. I find a few more pictures of the house and zoom in on one that seems to be the most recent. In the corner of the front window, there is a little blue sticker. I only see it because I'm looking for it. I've seen them before. Those little blue stickers are the packaging stickers that come with user-friendly security cameras for your home. You can put them up all over the house if you so desire, and the feed goes straight to your account on whatever device you have it on. It records, saves video, and can even alert you to motion. There will be no going into Stewart's house for reconnaissance.

I push back the chair from the computer and take a deep breath. What have I learned? Stewart's story about Angela checks out. I did fulfill that hit on her, and it was a clean hit. Stewart is also loaded with money, meaning he's not eager to get this cash back but not above hiring someone else. I'm starting to run out of options that sound good here, and I don't like that.

Plus, I can't shake the feeling that Henry and I are in danger.

Chapter 23

—◆—

HENRY WAKES ME up the following Sunday with a mug of something steaming. "No more wallowing," he says. "Get up, take a shower, and get dressed. We're going to do something normal. We're going to breakfast, and then we're going to the grocery store."

It's been just over a week since Stewart Houston dropped that envelope on the center console of his car. I know the time is coming to make a decision before Stewart makes it for me. Every day I spend time trying to figure out how to make this disappear, and every day, I come up with nothing. I still have no idea what to do next.

Henry is right. This kind of thinking is not working for anyone.

I get out of bed and follow the steps my husband laid out. The shower makes me feel more normal, at least for the time I'm in it. Hot water belts down on my head, and I imagine it can take all my problems and concerns down the drain with it. Which makes it seem laughable when it collects around my feet a little. The metaphor I was trying to employ here would mean that some of my problems are sticking around.

I wrench the shower off, wrap a towel around my body and my hair, and step into the bedroom. Henry smiles at me. "Beautiful. Feel better?" I groan in response and make my way to my closet to select some clothes.

From the dresser, I hear a faint vibrating. I nestled my most recent prepaid cell phone there among socks two days ago. I haven't been answering it. I don't want to take another job right now, not when I have to figure out how to do this one. I also don't want to talk to Stewart, and he's already proven he has a knack for finding my prepaid numbers. Honestly, I thought the device was powered off. I ignore it.

I slip into a clean pair of underwear and my favorite jeans. I put on a bra, and then I hear the phone ringing again. I pull it out, intending to power it down.

Henry appears in the doorway.

I jump, startled to be caught with this device literally in my hand. I put the phone behind my back. Immediately, I regret that choice. That's what guilty people with something to hide do. "You scared me," I say.

"I just need my shoes." Henry points to the floor on my left, where his shoes are lined up like a parade route.

"Right, sorry." I step out of the way, dropping the phone into the back pocket of my jeans as I do. I feel the vibration come to an end.

Henry stands up, a pair of sneakers in his hand. "You want to tell me what you hid behind your back there?" he asks. He looks tired, frustrated. This is not a conversation he wants to be having any more than I want to have it.

"Nothing."

The lie physically hurts. I feel like I swallowed a ball of

fire and tears prickle my eyes.

He steps closer, puts his free hand on my shoulder, and sighs. "Regina, I love you. Nothing you hid behind you is going to change that. I wish you would believe me. But these lies and secrets... They're starting to come between us. You feel that, right?"

The truth hurts, and I can't do anything but nod at him. How can I tell him about this? I can't. He can tell me that it won't change anything, but he's wrong. Obviously, this one secret changes everything we have built. "There's nothing you need to worry about," I say. "Everything is going to be fine."

I wonder if he may have believed me, melted into the hug I was trying to offer. I don't get to find out because the phone I slipped into my pocket chooses that moment to start another round of vibrations. Henry, his hand on my shoulder, feels it. Or maybe he hears it, the vibrations soft in the quiet closet.

Henry's hand slides down my back and into the pocket of my jeans. I watch the pain fill his expression when his hand closes around what he must recognize as the shape of a cell phone. I wonder what he thinks this could mean. He pulls it out of the pocket and holds it between us. I expect him to yell, but that's not Henry's style. Instead, his voice is whisper soft. "What the hell is this?"

A single tear slips down my cheek. I don't answer because to answer would be to admit too much.

"Answer it," he says. I shake my head. No, I don't want to answer it. I don't know how to explain to him why I can't answer it without giving too much away.

Right this moment, I hate myself with a passion that would make Stewart's request so simple. I have hidden this from every person in my life since I was a teenager. I have been so careful. Now this one moment will define everything that comes after it. This is the moment where the most important person in my life realizes more than I wanted him to. More tears slide down my face.

Henry slides his thumb into the phone and flips it open. "No," I say. But I say it too quietly; it lacks force. I'm easy to ignore. He puts the phone to his ear. "Who is this?" he says.

The closet is silent, and Henry is standing very close. I hear the voice answer. "Why, Henry. What a surprise. How are you this fine morning?"

Confusion pulls my husband's eyebrows together. "Who the fuck is this?" he asks, his voice rising.

"Calm down. This is Stewart. I'm a friend of Regina's. Well, friend isn't the right word, I suppose. I'm her employer, her client. She has a lot of my money, and I'm waiting to hear an update on a job I asked her to do."

The words have Henry's eyes going wide. He's connecting dots.

I reach up my hand toward the phone. "No," I say again.

Henry takes a step backward. "You're the one who asked her to do something illegal."

From the other end of the phone, I hear Stewart's laughter. "That's one way to put it, my friend. Oh, but the conversation you two will have to have tonight should be interesting. You make sure to ask her about Angela, will you? Then you tell her to call me with her update as soon as she possibly can. Have a good weekend, Henry."

Henry snaps the phone shut and tosses it on the floor. "What the hell was that?" I don't answer, can't seem to find my voice. I also can't seem to figure out something to tell him that isn't technically a lie but will allow me to fix this. "Regina, who is Stewart? Who is Angela? Where did this phone come from?"

I open my mouth, not sure what will come out, then snap it shut again.

"Say something," he yells. His voice echoes off the walls of the confined space.

"I can't," I yell right back at him. "I can't say anything without saying everything."

He shakes his head. I can tell he is grinding his teeth; it's a terrible habit Henry has when he's stressed. We joke about it sometimes, but obviously not right now. I keep the observation to myself. "So say everything." He gestures to the cell phone. "No more secrets. It's time."

I let the tears flow openly now, feel them dripping off my chin and onto my bare chest and rolling down my skin to the bra I'm wearing. "Nothing will ever be the same if I do that," I say. I drop my chin, not wanting to look at his face. I don't want to see the pain I'm causing him. I don't want to face this.

We stand there, frozen, for a few breath cycles. The silence feels heavy and oppressive. This entire moment feels charged, like it might explode any second. Then I feel Henry's fingers under my chin, pushing up. I let him pull my face to him. He kisses me gently. "This—whatever this is—is too much for you right now. I tried to give you space to deal with it, but it's crushing you. Don't you see that?" I nod. "Share it with me. I can help carry this burden. You're in trouble, Regina. It's time to let me in."

Chapter 24

I TAKE HENRY'S hand and lead him to the bed. I put a sweatshirt, left hanging over a chair last night, over my bra. Then I sit beside him. "I'm going to try and tell you the truth. It's not going to be easy for you to hear, and it's not going to be easy for me to say. There are things about me that you don't know." I grab his hand. "But I'm still me, I promise. This is the only thing I have ever kept from you." I gulp down my hesitation and power through. "But it's a big thing."

Henry nods, and I sigh. "I'm just going to sort of say the big part and let you hear it. You're going to have a lot of questions." Henry nods again. He's waiting for me to shatter his world. I know part of him probably thinks I'm being dramatic, that it isn't as bad as he's thinking. I wish he was right.

I take a deep breath and close my eyes so I don't have to watch his face. "People pay me to kill other people." This is the first time in my entire life I have said that sentence out loud. Henry is officially the first person I have ever told.

I open my eyes when there is no response from my husband. He is sitting in exactly the same position, but his eyes are narrowed in confusion. "Like a hitman?" he asks.

I shrug. Seems as good a word as any. "Angela, the person that the caller mentioned on the phone, was a mark I made a few years ago. Her boyfriend paid me money to have her killed."

Henry's hand flies to his mouth. "Oh my God, you're serious?"

I nod. "Do you want to know any of the details?"

He vehemently shakes his head. "No, I don't think that's a good idea." He closes his eyes, turns his head a little, and takes a deep breath. When he turns back to me and opens them again, he looks a little more calm. A little less like he is getting ready to puke. "You killed this Angela person? You actually killed her? You actually took the life of another human being?"

I nod. Technically, yes, I did. I've never admitted that to anyone before, either. It feels huge. I don't think I realized these truths were a sort of burden before. It's ridiculous, but I almost feel lighter. Shouldn't I feel more burdened? My husband will never look at me the same way again. He's probably going to leave me. He's certainly going to call the police. I should be worried about all of these consequences.

"How many people have you ..." He trails off, scared of the word. Or maybe he couldn't pick one: killed, murdered, been paid for?

"I don't know," I answer honestly. "I can estimate I've been paid for around fifty."

"Where is the money?" he asks. I think that's an odd next step, but I suppose it's a safe one for him to tread. Money is something we can talk about.

"Bank accounts, mostly. I have a few different ones. There's some cash in the house."

"And this is what that guy Stewart wants you to do? He wants you to kill someone?" Henry asks.

Shit. Yes, that's right. The entire reason we're having this little come-to-Jesus moment where I admit everything is because of that rat bastard, Stewart. I sigh and stand up from the bed. I go back into the closet and fetch the black duffle bag from where I stashed it under a spare blanket. I bring it to the bed and drop it beside Henry. "That's the money Stewart gave me for the hit. The way it works is they give me a single picture of the mark with the name in an envelope. I basically agree to do it by taking the money before I know who the mark is. Then I do my research into the mark and the client. Stop me if I'm giving you too much information," I say.

Henry shakes his head. "No, keep going."

"So Stewart tried to meet with me once before. I didn't like his vibe. He kept trying to control the situation, and I don't like that. I like to be in control."

Henry laughs. A real laugh. It feels somehow completely appropriate for this ridiculous conversation and makes me want to hug him. The fact that I'm not sure I'm allowed to makes me sad. He reaches for the duffle bag, pinching the zipper in his fingers. "Can I?" he asks.

"Please."

He unzips the bag, and his breath catches. "Holy shit."

"Yeah, that's a lot. Should be three hundred and fifty thousand dollars."

"Is that what you normally get?" he asks, his eyes still locked on the money. It's a lot of cash; it's mesmerizing.

Now it's my turn to laugh, a little one. "No. Not even close." That brings his eyes back to my face again. "He offered to triple my usual fee because he was desperate. He said it was personal."

"Your normal fee is one hundred thousand dollars?" His eyes are wide, his voice filled with reverence.

"No. I don't really have a normal. I sort of base it on the mark and what they look like they'll pay." I shrug. "It's not an exact science." I'm getting off the point again. I shake my head. "It doesn't matter. The point is Stewart made the offer to triple the fee, and he looked like he was worth a lot of money, so I aimed high. He hit that amount plus a fifty thousand dollar bonus, of sorts."

"So, what's the problem?" Henry asks. Then he groans in frustration. "God, I can't believe we're talking about this. But it sounds like he asked you to do something you've done before." He holds up a single finger, and his eyes narrow. "For the record, we're coming back to what the fuck it is you do for a living once I've wrapped my head around it."

"Ok." My voice shakes a little. There's the anger I was expecting, exploding out of his mouth for just a second. It makes my eyes water, but I hold back the tears.

"What about this job made it something you can't do?" he asks, gesturing to the bag.

"Here, I'll show you." I get up and go to the desk. I rustle around in the files in the back, the ones that normally hold bills and things. I pull up the single picture and drop it on the bed in front of him. Then I cautiously sit back down.

Henry stares at the picture, confused. He grabs it, just barely pinching the edge like it might burn him if he touches too much of it. He pulls it to his face, squinting. "Is that …" he trails off, pulling the picture even closer to his face. "What the fuck?"

he whispers.

"It's me."

He drops the picture. "What kind of a sick joke is that?"

I shake my head, tears pooling near my eyelids. "That was my exact reaction. But he's serious. The guy who called, Stewart, he's serious. He hired a private investigator after his sister died. He found a way to connect me to what happened."

Henry closes his eyes as if that information pains him. I rush on. "He's threatening to take it all to the police if I don't finish the hit. I'm worried he might come after you."

"You have to give the money back," Henry says. His voice is quiet, and his eyes are still closed. "Tell him it's not going to happen."

"I tried that."

Henry's eyes pop open. "What does he have? What proof?"

I shrug. "I don't know for sure. I know he has a picture that looks like it might be me meeting with the client who ordered the hit. He may have audio recordings of me talking to him. But I'm always careful. There's no way he has me saying anything specific. No way he can prove anything. At least, I don't think so."

It's the thinking that scares me. If I put too much energy into thinking about where I may have made a mistake, it gives me cramps in my stomach. My entire life has been about running from this, keeping this a secret, because I know what it looks like and how it's perceived. All of a sudden, someone knows. Really, two people know. The question is, what are they going to do with it?

I drop my head into my hands and close my eyes.

"Nothing is ever going to be the same again," I whisper.

I feel Henry's hand on my back, and I look up at his face. He's silently crying, tears slipping down his cheeks. "This is big. I can't believe you never told me. You've been doing this dangerous work, literally killing people, and you never told me. Are they...are they bad people?" He shakes his head. "It doesn't matter, does it? You don't have the right to..." He pulls his hand away from me, runs it down his face. "But you know you don't have that right. That's why you hid it. That's why this is so bad." His eyes land on my face, trapping me. "You might go to jail."

I let my long fingers frame my face. "I know." I guess part of me always knew that was a possibility. "I'll make sure you have all the account information, but try to keep it as quiet as you can for as long as you can. As soon as you start spending that money, they'll know about the accounts. They'll come for them. Maybe I should cash them out, give you the money to squirrel away somewhere. I want you to be able to take care of everything."

"Shit, Regina. Stop."

I bite my lip, stopping the words that had been tumbling out of my mouth.

"You're not the person I thought you were, are you?"

I nod. "I am. I swear. I'm the same wine drinking person I was before. I really do freelance work for IT companies. But..." I swallow. "There's something addicting about watching someone's soul leave them. I needed to find a way to see it without...without being a terrible person." I cover my face again. "Fuck, I'm doing a bad job of explaining this."

"Try," he says. "No point in holding it all in now."

"The marks are all vetted. I don't do it if they're not bad

people in some way. Cheaters, thieves, liars. They're people who are guilty of something. The people who hire me, they'd find another way if I left them alone. They'll find someone else. When I do it, I can do it right. I can do it carefully and..."

"You can see it happen," he says. There's a note of disgust in his voice. It makes me pull my head away from my hands and look at him. He looks angry. He is angry, I'm sure.

"Yeah, I guess."

"Ok." He throws his arms out, shaking them. "Listen for a second." I nod. "You fit those requirements, too, whether you like it or not. If you were a regular mark, you'd take the money and do the job."

"I suppose."

"You would, and I don't think you'd even hesitate," he says. His voice is hard, angry. "You just called these people bad people because they lie. Guess what, honey? You fucking lied for our entire marriage."

That hurts. I blink like he slapped me. He keeps going. "You'd see a mark, or whatever you called them, has fucking killed someone, and you wouldn't even hesitate. Go ahead, try and tell me I'm wrong. I'll wait."

I shake my head because we both know I can't find the flaw in that.

"Fine. Then here's what I need to know before we go any further." He leans toward me, bringing his face close to mine. "Do we have any more secrets I should know?"

"What? No. What the hell else would I be hiding?"

"Am I in danger?" he asks.

I blink. "What? From Stewart, maybe."

He shakes his head, moves in even closer. "From you.

Am I in danger now that I know?"

"No. Of course not." I can't even believe he thought that. "Are you going to leave me?" I whisper. "Or tell someone?"

He sighs. "I don't know yet. But first, we need to help you get out of this. I think I have an idea."

Chapter 25

HENRY'S PLAN IS a good one. Rough but workable. It turns out he can spin a story as well as I can.

Step one, buy more time. I pick up the disposable cell phone from the floor and dial the last number received. It rings three times before someone picks up without saying a word.

"Stewart, it's Regina," I say. Henry nods his approval. "You can't call me again. I told you, no more contact."

"You also told me you would do this, or I could go to the cops," he says. His voice drips like honey, like he is in control. Which, I suppose, he is. "You're out of time, little lady."

"Just a little more. Give me forty-eight hours."

"You're planning on taking care of this in the next two days?" He sounds skeptical. I can practically see his eyebrows rising up into his hairline.

"What's the point anymore?" I whine. "Henry knows everything. My life is over already." I'm not really faking the exhaustion and stress that find their way into my voice. I guess this is the new me, exposed and raw.

"He may as well get a sweet payday," Stewart says, his voice rising like a question.

"Exactly. Yes."

In front of me, Henry's eyes widen in question. "Fine. Two days," Stewart says. I give Henry a thumbs-up, and he pumps his fist in silent celebration. "But Regina, my dear?"

"What?"

"Don't let me down." His voice is harsh and angry. It's the first time I've ever heard Stewart Houston sound scary. I pull back the phone and look at it in shock. I'm watching when the screen changes back to the time, telling me he disconnected the call.

"We have forty-eight hours," I tell Henry.

"Then we better move fast," he says.

Doing research with Henry beside me is infinitely better than doing it alone. I'd like to tell you that he relaxed, but the tightness in his shoulders would prove I was lying. He kept a distance between our bodies the entire time, even though we were sharing a laptop. He would point to my screen without leaning his arm on mine. He would lean in to squint at something without letting our legs touch. I was shockingly aware of the absence of his touch, as though his touch was water, and he was intentionally letting me dehydrate.

At one point, Henry had the laptop on his lap and wanted to show me something on the screen. Although he angled it toward me a little, I used the opportunity to lean in. I pushed my left leg up against his as I craned my neck down to the device. When I sat back up, I left it there. Henry looked down at our legs and immediately stood up. "I'm getting some water," he said.

I slid the laptop over so it was in front of me and engrossed myself in memorizing details. In that way, I could almost ignore the fact that he came back with one glass of water and sat with his body a little further to the left. That told me more than I wanted to know about how much this hurt him. Henry two days ago would have offered me a glass of water. Henry two days ago would have brought me one. Henry two days ago would never have wanted extra space between us.

I'd broken our marriage.

Step two of the plan needed to go off that night. We only had forty-eight hours, so everything had to move fast. I slipped into a pair of jeans, the black hoodie, and a black hat. Henry did likewise, although his hat did have the typical home team B on the front. We drove in excruciating silence, Henry behind the wheel.

At my feet was the now infamous bag. This was easily the longest I had gone in my career without unpacking a bag of this nature. Three hundred and fifty thousand dollars, although I still had yet to verify that. I felt like I had been lugging this bag all over the state since acquiring it. Definitely not my normal modus operandi. If we were pulled over for running a red light or speeding, this bag could be a little difficult to explain. I don't mention that to Henry.

His jaw is clenched as he drives, and his thumbs are lightly tapping out the rhythm of the song playing lightly on the radio. He is staring straight ahead, focused. To anyone else, this may look typical, but I know Henry. I know his brain is running through our past and tapping on memories that feel like bruises right now. He's finding flaws in the life we have built together.

Part of me knows I have to let him work through this, let him decide if what he now knows is forgivable. Part of me wants to give him all the reasons why it is, make the decision for him. I wisely keep silent.

The house we're looking for is not the biggest house on the street but it is on a corner, which makes its side yard larger than most of the others. It's also fenced-in, which gives it better curb appeal. These houses are closer together than the ones in our neighborhood, the result of trying to cram more living spaces into less area because we're closer to the city. But this one has a driveway, where most don't. Henry drives past the house, and I note the single car in the driveway, a black Infinity. "He's home," I say.

"Good." That single word is all I get before Henry makes a right on Grozier Road.

The right side of the house sits on a one-way street but has the largest probability of staying off the home's cameras. That little extra side yard helps the owner with privacy, and he's done a decent job of cultivating large trees to hide his house from the rest on this side. That is our best bet. Which means we have to come at that street the same way we just came at it since it's one way.

We have to take the long route around, a quarter of a mile down this road which is residential and requires Henry to drive slowly. Then a right turn onto an expressway which will let him drive a little faster for another quarter mile. That puts us back on Huron Avenue, approaching the one-way street. Henry drives it all expertly, exactly like he mapped out from the virtual maps at home. He keeps the red needle of the car pointed perfectly at the speed limits on all the roads. He turns right onto Larch Road and pulls immediately to the inlet in the curb. There's a no parking sign here, but he's not parking.

We both look around the neighborhood, checking for

nosy neighbors or people out for a stroll. Normally, when I do this kind of job, I'm trying to be invisible. This is another first for me: the first time I've ever wanted to be seen.

"There's a lady up ahead, coming this way," Henry says.

I follow the direction he appears to be looking and see what he sees. She's walking a little dog, and she's on her phone. "Perfect," I whisper.

I open the car door and take my time wrapping my hand around the handles of the bag, letting the dome light from inside the car spill out onto the street longer than I should. Then I slam the door. A smile dances on my lips when the sound bounces off the two-story houses surrounding us. Do I have your attention now, dog walker?

I cross in front of the car, right through the headlights, and straight up to the property. I make a show of looking around, left-right-left-right-left, with big head motions. Then I stand on my tiptoes and lower the bag over the wooden fence and into the yard.

The last thing I do is run the distance back to the car, jump inside, tell Henry to "GO" like they do in the movies, and slam the door. Henry peels away from the curb and drives back toward the expressway.

I turn around and see the woman inspecting what we've left behind.

"Did it work?" he asks.

"She definitely sees it."

"Good." He clears his throat. "Do you...do you plan on stopping after this one job is done?" he asks.

It's the first time he's mentioned any sort of future after this situation. The first time he's tried to get me thinking like there is an after-this-job version of me. I don't want to keep secrets from him, not anymore. I want to be honest with him. I want to be able to tell Henry the truth. "I can try," I say honestly. "I want to try for you."

He shakes his head. "We don't even know if you will be around to try anything else," he says. "It's Stewart's move now. We have to see which way he goes."

When it falls silent in the car again, I try to imagine Stewart being alerted to the strange bag on his property. I imagine him recognizing the bag immediately but trying to pretend he doesn't. I imagine him walking slowly toward it, unzipping the bag, and finding the cash he gave me. I wonder how long it takes him to notice the white index card we've left on top. The one with my careful handwriting. The one that says, "Let this be the end of the conversation, or no one will miss you."

Your move, Mr. Houston.

Chapter 26

HENRY PULLS THE car into the garage and pushes the remote button to return the garage door to its closed position. "It's late. I'm going to bed," he says. He turns the car off and opens the door but doesn't get out. I have the sense he's waiting for something. "Regina?"

"What?"

"Where are you sleeping tonight?"

Oh, that hurts. My throat burns so suddenly, I have to swallow twice before I can find the words. "I'll sleep on the couch, of course."

"Great." He gets out and slams the car door. I let him go.

I sit in the car until the light inside the garage turns off, plunging me into darkness. Then I open the car door, using the dome light to check that my path is clear. After I close the door, I walk quickly before my brain can forget the route.

Henry, in more passive-aggressive displays of his anger, has left all the lights off in the house as well. But we have windows that let in a little of the light from the moon, and I can see the floor here better than I could in the garage. I pad my way across the house and up the stairs to the bedroom, where Henry has flipped on the television.

I get changed into my pajamas in my closet by the light of the nightly news. I hear Henry running water in the bathroom sink. Then I hear the bathroom door open. I wait in the closet, wondering if he's about to come in to change into his pajamas. I wonder if I should be here, maybe standing topless to seduce him. Maybe I should be gone, left already for my new accommodations in the living room.

In the end, it doesn't matter. I hear the creaking of the bed and know that he's not coming into the closet. He must have changed before I came in from the garage.

I take a single blanket from the chest at the foot of the bed and head for the family room. I want him to sit up in bed and tell me to stop. I want him to invite me to come talk to him, really talk. I want him to follow me, maybe even yell at me. I want him to show some emotion. Emotion I can work with. This lack of emotion is the scariest thing. This tells me he is giving up. How can I work with giving up?

The couch is cold when I drop my body onto it. We made a choice to buy a microfiber couch when we first got this place. Normally, I love it. But the material doesn't hold warmth, so I can feel the cold seeping into my skin. I wrap the blanket around my body like I'm swaddling an infant and try again. It's a little warmer, but I'm sacrificing the ability to move my body. It will have to work.

My sleep is restless and intermittent. I drift off for about an hour and then wake up because a limb has fallen asleep, I'm too close to the edge of the couch, or I have a crick in my neck. Then I remedy the issue and repeat.

At some point, when I've repeated the waking cycle maybe four times, I hear the crunch of tires nearby. I hear a door slam and footsteps approaching the house. I lay there, blinking in the darkness, waiting for the knock I already know is coming. It takes longer than it should. I wonder if there was a pause to look for a car or maybe glance in a window. Finally, it comes. The knock. Three short but unmistakable raps on the door jam.

I give it a second, despite how close I am to the door. I tell myself the story. I was deeply asleep and had a moment of panic when I heard the knock. I wasn't expecting it; it dragged me from a good dream, startled me. I don't rub my eyes. Instead, I let them droop to half-mast.

Henry appears in the doorway, looking bedraggled and exhausted. "Blanket," he whispers. Right, appearances. I drape the blanket I had been using over the back of the couch, making it look like it is awaiting use by someone watching television. Then I fluff up the couch pillow I had used for my head and toss it into the corner of the sofa, where it normally sits.

Henry waits for me to finish all this preparation, then he unlocks the heavy wooden front door and pulls it open. There is a state police officer, wearing a blue button-down uniform shirt, standing on my front patio. He shines a flashlight into the room. Henry holds up his arm, squinting in the light. "Sorry." Henry flips the porch light on, and the flashlight turns off. "Can we help you?" Henry asks. He's either a good actor, or he really was asleep. His annoyance is dripping from each word.

"I'm looking for Regina. Is she here?" the officer asks.

I step beside my husband. "I'm Regina."

"What's this about?" Henry asks, throwing his arm across the frame as if keeping us separated from each other is important.

"We just have a few quick questions for Regina. Do you think I could step inside? It's chilly out here today."

This man is not a detective. He's a patrol officer. He's responding to a routine call, perhaps one that showed no real danger. He's taking a statement. The odds are low that he is here to arrest me. That tells me Stewart didn't go with the "turn over everything I have" option today. I tap Henry on the shoulder, a silent signal. He drops his arm and steps back. "Of course. Come in."

The officer steps into the front room, and Henry shuts the door. I flip the light switch that will allow light to flood the room. "What is so important that it couldn't wait until the sun came up?" Henry asks.

"Regina, where were you around ten o'clock tonight?"

I shrug. "With Henry."

The officer's eyes flick to Henry. "Are you Henry?" My husband nods in agreement. Eyes back to me now. "Where exactly were the two of you at that time?"

"Just out for a drive," I say.

"Were you, perhaps, anywhere near Huron Avenue tonight?"

I flash Henry a look that is, perhaps, a little guilty. "Maybe," I say. My voice quavers a little.

The officer sighs. "I'm going to level with you because it's late, and I'm tired. Do you know a man named Stewart Houston?"

"Sounds familiar," I answer. "Does he work for Innovative IT Solutions? I do freelance work for them sometimes."

The officer nods. "That's him." He smiles at me. "You're not a fan of his, I take it? Or maybe not a fan of the sort of things he asks you to do in your freelance work?"

Henry shakes his head. "I told you they'd trace this back to us."

The officer holds out his hand. "Now wait a second. Unless you answer these few questions, I don't fully know what we're dealing with. Calm down." He's speaking to Henry, who nods. Back to me again. "Did Mr. Houston offer you some money for some kind of freelance job?"

That's information he must have received from Stewart. I wonder if Stewart said "freelance" or if this statey is filling in the details with what I just gave him. Either way, it works.

"Yes, but I couldn't do it." I look at Henry, which makes it easy to let my eyes fill with water. "I didn't want to do it. What he's asking me to do... It's not right."

"Did you do anything illegal? Did you do any part of the job?"

I widen my eyes, shocked. "No, of course not. But he gave me the money anyway."

He takes a notebook out of his pocket, flips to a page. There's no pen. He's reading, not recording. "Three hundred and fifty thousand dollars?" he asks, still looking at the paper.

"Is that how much was in there?" I lay my hand on my chest. "Oh my God, I didn't count it or anything. That's a lot of money. Are you sure it was that much?"

He shuts the notebooks, puts it back in his pocket. "So you and Henry drove to Mr. Houston's house and returned the money?" he asks.

"That was my idea," Henry says. The officer turns his

head to look at my husband. "She was really upset about the job before that money showed up. Then she was adamant that the money must have been from this guy. So we decided to just return it."

"And the threat inside? Was that your idea as well?"

Time to play up on his assumptions. See, the thing about patrol officers like this is they play the odds. They have to make fast decisions, think on their feet. This guy is assuming the threat of violence was Henry's idea because in most situations, it would be the male who is more prone to violence. Obviously, I'm the exception to this rule. But he doesn't know that.

I take a step toward my husband, anger showing on my face. "Threat? What is he talking about, Henry?"

Henry holds up his hands. "It was nothing. Just a paper. I may have told him no one would miss him or something vague like that." Henry turns to the officer. "I obviously didn't mean it. I was just trying to scare him."

"Alright." The officer takes a deep breath. "I don't like this, but here's where we are. Mr. Houston says the money is his. He tried to pay you to do a job, and you refused to do it and returned the money. That matches with what you're telling me. It's not a crime to return his money. The threat could be..." He pauses long enough to level a serious gaze at Henry. "But Mr. Houston has kindly decided not to press charges for that."

Henry breathes a sigh of relief.

"Now you mentioned the thing he asked you to do was illegal. That is something we should look into. Would you be willing to give more information to a detective?" he asks, looking at me again.

"I don't know. Maybe."

"Alright, it's late. We don't need to decide this today. I'm going to pass along your information to a detective. They'll contact you in the next few days." He takes a step toward the door. Henry, who is standing beside it, opens it for him. "You two have a nice evening, and stay away from Mr. Houston."

"Of course."

He steps outside and turns back around. "I'm serious. No phone, no visits, no contact with Mr. Houston."

"We got it, Officer. Thank you," Henry says.

"And Regina?" the officer prompts. "Next time someone drops that much money at your feet, you call us immediately. Are we clear?"

"Absolutely, Officer. I'm sorry for the trouble."

Henry shuts the door. I stand beside him, listening for the sounds of the footsteps. I hear them pause. I know that means the officer is still standing there. Henry opens his mouth, and I hold up my hand, silencing him. I shake my head and point to the door.

Then I walk purposely to the light switch, flip it off, and motion for my husband to follow me. I walk to the other side of the house, up the stairs, and into our bedroom. When Henry follows me in, I shut the door and flip on the light. "Sorry for shushing you. He was still there. Maybe he was listening, I don't know."

"So Stewart called the police, just like you thought he would," Henry says.

I nod. "But he didn't turn over any other evidence. Which means either he doesn't really have any—"

"Which is unlikely," Henry adds.

"Or he's not planning on turning any of it over."

It was a dangerous step of the plan, calling Stewart's bluff. But it was a risk I was willing to take once Henry knew. I think Stewart was always planning to use Henry as the lynch pin, the one person I would do anything to protect from the information. Whatever he has, I don't think it's enough for the police. This act of bringing the police down on his doorstep proved that. If he was going to turn something in, he would have done it tonight. The bag full of cash would have only served as further proof.

"Does it seem like he took it easy on you?" Henry asks. "On the TV shows, cops are always pushy. They don't let anything go that easily."

I laugh lightly. "On the TV shows, the script tells them this is the bad guy. Real life isn't that simple. That guy doesn't know who I am; he only knows what Stewart told him and what I just told him. He knows you and I are white. Based on where we live, he also knows we're upper middle class at the very least. The fact that he didn't treat me like a criminal doesn't mean he doesn't think I am one. It just means he's thinking Stewart is a little sketchy and strange. That's good for us."

"So do you think there's a chance this is over?" Henry asks. The naive part of my husband, the part that knew nothing about this world and is still terrible at predicting it, wants it to be this simple.

I almost wish there was a part of me who could let him continue to live in that world. "No. No way he makes it that easy. He'll find a way to up the stakes. I'm sure of it."

Chapter 27

DESPITE THE INTERRUPTION in the middle of the night, Henry insists on waking up to the same 6:30 alarm clock he always uses. I hear him come out of the bedroom and start grinding coffee beans. I stay where I am on the couch among the blankets, wondering if he is making a full pot or a half. Does finding out your wife kills people for a living negate making her a cup of coffee?

I listen to the sounds of his normal morning routine. I've watched it so many times that the sounds tell me exactly what is happening. I close my eyes and visualize it. He packs a quick lunch, leftovers of some kind, into a lunch box. Zips it closed. Pours the coffee into a travel mug, screws on the lid. Walks across the flooring to the bathroom. Leaves the water running while he brushes his teeth. Slams the door to the bedroom on his way out. Grabs everything and heads for the garage door.

I hear his footsteps hesitate and imagine that he's in the doorway to the family room. Is he wondering if he should say something? Wondering if I'm asleep?

Eventually, I hear the sound of the door to the garage slam and the garage door rolling up. Then I throw the blanket off and get myself off the couch. I make my way to the kitchen and check the carafe. I feel a ball of complex emotions when I see the black liquid reaches the two-cup line. Exactly the amount I would normally pour into my large mug. There's something in that small gesture that means the world to me. Yes, Henry makes coffee every day. Yes, he probably made it out of routine. But I know there was that moment of hesitation. I know he had a chance to do something petty and change this part of what he does. The fact that he chose not to means something. There's hope there in that carafe this morning.

I fill my favorite mug, spill in some creamer, and take the mug to the office.

There, I drop in front of the computer and open up all of my files. I still use the secure server, mostly because there could always be other eyes on this computer besides Henry's. I wade my way through all the old files from my past, looking for errors or important information. I delete a lot of things. Notes, client information, and altered images all get deleted.

I pause for lunch, eating a salad over the sink to make cleanup easier. When I drop back into the chair, I look over what I've been saving and delete all of it. Nothing from these past cases is worth keeping evidence of, even in the partition I've created on the hard drive. It's not Henry I'm worried about, not anymore.

When everything is gone, I open a command line interface. I stare at the black interface for a second, pausing to take a deep breath before I type anything. There is no way to undo what I'm about to do. I've spent years building this partition to be secure. My own little silent warehouse of information. Was it fallible? Sure, everything is. But it was as close to perfect as anything I've ever created.

Enough. I type the command that will delete the partition.

Then I write the script that will overwrite the unused space on the disk with random binary bits. I repeat it three times.

Any record of that partition is officially gone. Triple filled and overwritten by other random data.

I open a standard notes document, the kind used by every housewife across the country who doesn't know a single thing about computers. I type out bank account information for all of the accounts, mentally copied from one of the documents that no longer exists. I will have to figure out how to code these at some point. But Henry will have them all when he needs them. The only one I leave out is the one shared with the handler. That one he can empty as a final payment. It's the best I can do.

I check the clock. This trip down memory lane, erasing my footsteps as I go, has taken me all day. Henry will be home in forty-five minutes. Normally this is when I would push my chair back and make my way to the kitchen, prepare dinner. My feet itch to do just that.

I don't think I can, though. That picture of normal, that housewife image, it's all going to feel so fake to him right now. I don't know how to explain to him that both of those things he now pictures, the housewife pouring wine and stirring dinner and the killer standing over the body watching life leave someone's eyes, they're both me. I can be both of those people at the same time. Maybe I should have let him binge-watch that killer forensic pathologist show more after all.

I open a delivery app and click on a local restaurant. I

order a hummus platter, a pita platter, and a large salad. I can't order a bottle of wine for delivery from this particular restaurant, but I think I have a white that will go fine with this chilling in the refrigerator. I check the delivery time and click confirm.

There. No housewife prepping dinner but no murderous villain either. I'm just me, somewhere in the middle.

The delivery shows up five minutes after Henry would normally arrive home and about fifteen minutes before he actually does. When I hear the garage door, I prepare myself for another silent encounter. The food is lumped in the middle of the table, still in the delivery containers. I've added plates and silverware beside it, but I have decided to forgo the serving bowls I would normally insist on using to make it seem more like a family dinner. I leave the bottle of wine in the fridge. Although it's part of my plan, I decide to let it seem more spontaneous when Henry comes in.

He opens the door and comes in like a storm. He's moving fast, his hair is disheveled, and he's carrying a large cardboard box which he drops to the floor with a bang that echoes through the room. He points to it, eyes flashing with something that almost looks like excitement. "Four hundred thousand," he says.

"What?"

"Four hundred fucking thousand dollars. I verified it myself after we closed. You were right."

I get up and cross to the box. It's filled with bank-wrapped hundred-dollar bills. A lot of them. I touch Henry's arm. "Where did this come from?" I ask, my voice quiet. He doesn't pull away from me.

"It was delivered to the bank this afternoon. No return

address, just a courier service. It's addressed to me." He pushes one flap up with his foot so I can see the sticker with Henry's name and the bank address. He reaches into his pocket and produces a small index card. "This was inside."

For you in your time of grief. Spend wisely. SH

"SH," I say, shaking my head. "He's not being very subtle, is he?"

Henry pockets the index card again. "He's appealing to me. He thinks, in my anger, I'll talk you into doing what he wants you to do. He thinks I want you dead as much as he does."

My intake of breath sounds shaky, even to my own ears. "Do you?"

His eyes lock onto mine, and emotions overwhelm me. Henry has a lot of emotion; he always has. I think that's part of why I fell in love with him. I have always struggled with emotions, and here is this guy who wears them on his face at all times. It's beautiful.

Right now, I see the war he's fighting with himself. I see anger but I also see love. He doesn't have all these answers either. I almost burst into tears when he touches my arm. I knew I was craving that touch, and I push my arm right back into his palm, maximizing it.

"Never," he whispers. "I don't know a lot right now, but I know more death is not something I'm looking forward to."

"Ok." It's not a satisfactory answer to such a proclamation, but it's the best I can choke out without tears following it.

"Did you take care of the files like you said you needed to?" he asks.

I just nod. He doesn't want the details. "Are you

hungry?" I tip my head toward the table full of food. Now it's Henry's turn to nod. He slips out of his jacket, letting it fall to cover the box full of cash on the floor. Then he sits at the table and reaches for a plate.

"Wine?" I ask. "I have white in the fridge."

Henry puts the second plate in front of my usual spot. "Wine would be great," he says. "We have to talk about the next part of the plan."

Right. The next part of the plan.

I head to the kitchen to retrieve the bottle of wine. Alcohol may be required for me to accept what has to happen next. It's not every day that I sit down to plan a death like this. Sure, I've planned lots of deaths. I've even planned some that look like suicides.

But I've never actually planned a suicide.

This one will be new.

Chapter 28

"I'M GOING TO bed," Henry says, punctuating the statement with a yawn. "It's been a long day, and we are just going in circles here." He stands up and stretches. "We'll figure out the details later. I'm sure you have plenty of ideas."

Somehow, the statement feels like a slap to the face. Plenty of ideas. Is that code for 'you've already done this enough'? Maybe I'm being too sensitive.

I pick up the wine glasses and the few napkins left on the table and take them all to the trash. "I'm on the couch," I say, although we both already knew that. Henry just nods. I toss the napkins in the trash and set the wine glasses on the counter.

Then my phone rings. Not the disposable, which is on vibrate, but my personal cell phone. I cross to the charger and pick up the phone. The screen is displaying a number I don't recognize. I swipe it open. "Hello?"

"Regina King?" Deep male voice.

"This is Regina."

"This is Detective Peterson with the Massachusetts State Police. I was told to contact you regarding some information you may have about a crime."

I jog into the bedroom, flipping on the light. I point to the phone and mouth "Detective." This is an eventuality we discussed at dinner. That trooper was always going to reach out. The question was did he put the ball in my court, Stewart's court, or the detective's. I have to find out. "What?" I ask, sounding confused and a little tired.

"A trooper visited your house two nights ago. Do you recall that?"

"Yes, of course."

"He said you mentioned Stewart Houston may have asked you to do some freelance work that was something you simply couldn't do. He was under the impression it was something you may need to speak with me about. Is that ringing any bells, Regina?" Using my name is a strategy. He's trying to show me he's on my side.

I roll my eyes. "This is all getting completely out of hand," I say. I sigh loud enough for him to hear. "I just don't want to do the job for them. That's it. Let me just move on. I didn't take that money, and I didn't do anything."

He coughs a little. "Right, Regina, but if he is asking you to do something illegal—"

"Who said anything about illegal?" I bark, cutting him off. "Did he tell you that?"

"Is that not what we're talking about?" he asks. "Let's clear this up right now. Regina, what did Stewart ask you to do? What did he offer to pay you so much money for?"

I wink at Henry. This guy knows absolutely nothing. The ball is definitely in my court. "He asked me to try and get into his company server any way I can. That's what I do; I'm a cybersecurity expert. But then he asked me to wipe something from his employee record while I was inside the system. I told him no, I don't do that. I refuse to work with someone who expects all employees to just be at his beck and call. If he has something he needs changed, he needs to do it on the record in the right way."

There's silence on the other end of the line. The detective is likely weighing whether any of this is worth his time. "Let me get this straight. You're saying Stewart Houston offered you three hundred and fifty thousand dollars in cash just to take something off of his employee record?" Skepticism makes his voice heavy, and suddenly, he's the one that sounds exhausted.

"I don't know. I didn't count that money. The other officer told me how much it was, and I was shocked. That's so much money. Do you think maybe there's something really dangerous on his record? Maybe they have, like, a record of something he shouldn't have done?" I drop my voice to a stage whisper. "Did he commit a crime or something?"

"Did you try to access the information?" the detective asks, almost sounding hopeful now.

"No. No, of course not. I gave the money back, and I told the company I was out."

Again, the other end of the line is quiet for a beat. "Alright, I understand. Maybe I can get one of our guys to look into this from our end. Can I have someone contact you if they need more information?" he asks.

I smile at Henry, knowing that this future contact will never happen. But the idea is there now. The idea that Stewart may be the one hiding something. That's an idea we can absolutely use in our story. This is all good news.

"Of course," I say. "I'm glad you called. Thank you for

putting my mind at ease."

"You have a nice night," he says. "Good night."

"Good night." I hang up the phone and smile at Henry. "No problems. I think that's over. We are off the radar."

Henry smiles. "Sounds like Stewart isn't."

"No, it definitely doesn't sound like he is. Poor guy."

It feels so comfortable and relaxed right now. So comfortable that I forget it's not. I forget that Henry is standing in our bedroom in his pajama bottoms waiting for me to leave the bedroom. His eyes flit to the light switch as though he is realizing the same thing.

My smile falls, and I nod, just once. "Right. I'll let you get some sleep. See you in the morning."

I hit the light switch and turn out of the room. I want him to call for me to stop. I want him to have another question or to tell me it would be alright if I slept in the room. I want him to interact with me like he used to.

But he lets me pad my way down to the family room and lay down to sleep in total silence.

Chapter 29

THE ONE THING I know for certain about my own death is that I would like it to not be messy at all. There are a lot of ways to die. I personally have seen a lot of different deaths. Many of them leave a lot of clean up behind. When I'm in charge of planning a death, this isn't really something I consider. Sure, I'd like to stay clean myself, but the scene doesn't matter to me. I'm not the person who has to come in after the death and try and get all signs of the death out. But if it is my own death, my own important people cleaning after me, I'd like to consider that.

This rules out a lot of options, including the handgun, which is the most cliche method I could think of. I've actually only used a gun for a hit once in my career if you can believe that. For the record, I'm not counting William Archer. As I've already explained, he killed himself. I've been to the gun range. I'm actually a decent shot. But only once has it ever come down to me firing a gun. I try to find other, more creative ways.

Guns are traceable, for one. It's easy to match a bullet to the gun that fired it if you have the gun. They're also expensive, require your name to be put on a list, and take time to get your hands on. Plus, you have to have ammunition. Compare that to, say, a knife. A decent knife can be acquired at any number of stores without registration or waiting. They're cheap, easy to clean, and have hundreds or thousands exactly like them made every single day. No one looks twice at a woman of my age and social status popping into a store to pay cash for a knife. Everyone looks twice when it's a handgun. I own at least five different knives that would get the job done. I don't own a gun. But I digress. The point is that the handgun is out.

In fact, the knife is also out. While it would be incredibly easy to, say, slit my wrists in a tub, the process isn't guaranteed to get results. It would be possible to save my life at the hospital, which I can assume would negate the entire deal. Plus, that leaves a lot of mess behind later. There is no method of killing yourself, or someone else, with a knife that doesn't leave behind a lot of blood to clean up. So, the knife is out.

Poison, which you already know I'm familiar with, is tricky. Taking the right amount is the easy part. Vomiting can be contained, making it easier to clean. But, again, I run the risk of someone attempting a reversal that keeps me alive. Normally, I wouldn't have a problem with this. But Stewart doesn't seem like the type to accept an attempt on a hit as the full deal. This will need to be irreversible.

I do consider the idea of stealing right from the story Stewart has already heard. Closing my garage door while leaving my car running. I consider taking sleeping pills myself, so the process is basically painless. It seems poetic in a lot of ways. It also seems like another way to bring the police a connection to Stewart, one that detectives may already be looking for. In my line of work, connections drawn for the police tend to be avoided at all costs, so the poetic route is out.

That leaves me with basically two options, car accident and drowning. Both of those have the benefit of being things you automatically assume are accidents. Cars crash all the time, even on the road by themselves. It would be easy to drive my car off a cliff or into oncoming traffic. If I take careful precautions, I can make sure no innocent person is hurt along the way. Is there a clean up? Of course. But this clean up is done by professionals, not by people who loved me. The scene is not somewhere my Henry has to visit every day. It's not somewhere Henry is expected to live.

Drowning is interesting because it's not something one can do to themselves. Your brain loves itself entirely too much to let you drown it. Your reflexes will override every bit of common sense you have and keep you from actually dying by drowning. It's amazing. So this requires some way to keep the body underwater long enough for the job to be done.

Of course, one common way of making sure this happens is to combine the two. Car accidents in water are popular in movies and television. I happen to live near an ocean, lots of rivers, and a few lakes. Lack of water is not an issue. This has merit.

I stand up from the table and stretch my neck. You may be wondering how I'm staying so cool and calm about this. Essentially, I'm sitting at my own kitchen table, planning my suicide. Yes, but you have to remember this very important set of facts.

1. I have no choice.
2. Nothing is what it seems.

But we'll come back to that second one. For now, let me tell you the story I'm leaning towards.

Regina King was driving alone at night, south along state route 24. Water on the roadway caused her to lose traction, slamming through the small guardrail and into the water below. The driver hit her head during the crash, possibly leading to a loss of consciousness. The car then filled with water. Ultimately, the cause of death, in this case, is drowning.

Isn't that a deliciously simple story? Of course, I'll have to be there at night. I'll have to ensure the roadway is actually wet, which shouldn't be too difficult this time of year. I do believe it's even supposed to rain tonight. I will have to be driving fast enough to have the entire story be believable and to ensure that I do hit my head. Seatbelt will be off, of course, and the windows cracked a little to let in fresh air. That also has the added benefit of letting in the water fast to make sure there is no waking up before the water has done its thing. For extra protection, there is always that wonderful sleeping tablet which could be slipped under the tongue before the accident.

Still, that particular story leaves a lot of errors. If I can't bring myself to wrench the wheel, if I don't actually drown, if I don't hit my head just right to give the medical examiner reason to believe I may have passed out. There has to be another option.

There's always the quarries, I suppose. No driving near there, of course, but there is a forty-foot rock into the water where people drown all the time. You're not supposed to jump from the quarry; there's no swimming in the water. These are simple rules posted on signs for teenagers across the state to ignore. It's a popular spot to find people right at dusk or during the day. But at night, I would have the area to myself. Perhaps this story would be better.

Regina King became the most recent drowning death in the Milford quarries when she jumped from the rock ledge at night, breaking her neck. Don't jump from the quarries, kids. Trespassing in this area is illegal.

I like that one. The morality lesson is included for free.

The back door closes with a loud bang, and Henry comes into the room. "I'm having trouble with a satisfactory step three," I tell him. Step one: test Stewart's willingness to give information to the cops. Step two: wait for Stewart to step up his game, see if he involves Henry. Step three: Regina has to die.

"What have you come up with?" he asks, pouring himself a large glass of lemonade from the refrigerator. He is dripping with sweat, thanks to his desire to mow the entire back lawn by himself this afternoon. Normally, we bring someone in to do this. If I had to guess, I'd bet the decision is based on the fact that his salary alone may not have left enough money to consistently pay the yard guy. Meaning, in his mind, this is a service we paid for with blood money.

"Car accident on state 24, into the water."

He wrinkles his eyes at me. "Drowning?"

"Or jump into the quarry. Death with a lesson."

Henry shakes his head. "No." He gulps the lemonade,

draining the glass in one drink. Then he refills it, replaces the container, and comes into the dining room. He drops into the chair beside me and leans his elbows on the wooden table. "I have a much better idea."

I listen to his entire idea, helping fill in details only when he obviously doesn't understand the way real life works. We end up ordering pizza when we get hungry, then we rehash the plan again.

By the third time we've talked through it, I'm convinced. It's absolutely perfect.

Chapter 30

THE MORNING OF *August 15, Henry King left his home to head into the office at 7:15 AM. His wife, Regina King, was alone in their residence when he left. The two had recently had a few disagreements, and Regina was asleep on the couch in the living room. Mr. King was at work in the bank from 7:45 AM until 3:00 PM. Sworn statements from three employees and one customer can attest to this. In addition, Mr. King was on the bank's closed-circuit security cameras for most of the day.*

Mr. King returned to his residence at 3:30 PM and parked his car in the garage. Upon entering the residence through the door from the garage, Mr. King didn't immediately notice anything was wrong. It wasn't until he rounded the corner into the kitchen that he noticed things were not what they appeared.

The kitchen floor was smeared with blood, the back door was ajar, and there was no sign of his wife, Regina King, anywhere in the house. It was at this time, 3:37 according to call logs, that Mr. King called 9-1-1.

Police arrived on scene and put out a missing person

bulletin on Regina King. The blood on the scene was the same blood type as the missing person. A sweep of the property revealed a chef knife from the kitchen block in the backyard, the blade covered in blood that was a match to the blood found on the floor. Tire treads were found in the dirt along the side of the house, leading to the back fence, which was ajar. Those tire treads are not consistent with the ones on either of the vehicles owned by the Kings. The treads match an ultra-high-performance tire most commonly found on luxury SUVs or trucks.

Mr. King was brought in for questioning and ultimately released. His alibi at the bank, as well as his lack of access to vehicles that would utilize those tires, means he likely had nothing to do with his wife's disappearance. In addition, Mr. King has not recently made any large purchases, withdrawals, or deposits from his bank accounts.

In the late afternoon of August 16th, a press conference was held to discuss the missing person's case and urge the public to call the tip line if they had seen Regina King. The information about the tire treads was given as well as her last known location. Three hours after the conference aired, a phone call came in with a lead that sounded promising. A witness who preferred to remain anonymous but lived in a unit on Shadowbrook Lane reported seeing a strange car parked on the road on the afternoon of August 15th. The witness saw a woman who matched Regina's description being helped out of the passenger seat of the vehicle by a male. The two reportedly walked into the trees to the east of the property. The witness could not identify the make and model of the car except to say that it was a dark-colored SUV, possibly black.

Police traveled to the scene. Approximately 600 feet to the east of the location are the cliffs known as the Milford Quarry, a dangerous location. The quarry was searched for signs of a body, but none were found.

In the early evening of August 16th, Henry King called the police investigators to say that a threatening note had been found at his primary residence. He was unsure whether the note had been there prior to Regina's disappearance. He did not remember seeing the note before. The simple white index card read: "Do the job you were hired to do or no one will find the body." It was signed "SH". When asked who "SH" may be referring to, Henry explained that the police had been investigating some freelance work Stewart Houston may have tried to hire his wife to complete. He was unclear on the details of the freelance contract except to say that he was relatively certain Regina had not taken the job.

On the evening of August 16th, investigators went to the primary residence of Stewart Houston. A knock on the front door went unanswered. There was no visible car in the driveway and no lights on in the residence.

On August 17th, police went to the place of work for one Stewart Houston. It was there they learned Mr. Houston had not been seen at work since August 15th, when he left work around 1:00 in the afternoon. Calls to Mr. Houston's cell phone and residence had gone unanswered. A missing person's report was started for Mr. Houston, and an APB was put out for his car, a black Infiniti QX80. At this time, the police are considering him a person of interest.

Stewart Houston's vehicle was found in the economy parking lot of the Boston Logan International Airport on August 19th. No airline tickets were purchased in Mr. Houston's name from that airport in the month of August. There is no record of an airline ticket purchased from Mr. Houston bank in the last year. There was, however, a substantial cash withdrawal made in the last six months. Mr. Houston took five hundred thousand dollars from his savings account in January of this year.

Further investigation into Mr. Houston turned up a box of photos in his closet. These photos appear to be taken from some crime scenes in Massachusetts, including the suicide death of William Archer and of Mr. Houston's own sister Angela Ripple. Investigators are reopening those cases looking for evidence of foul play.

At this time, there have been no new developments in the case. Regina King is missing, presumed dead. Stewart Houston is still considered a person of interest in her disappearance. Anyone with any evidence is encouraged to call the Massachusetts State Police.

Chapter 31

HENRY KING SIGNS the deed, selling the gambrel house for four hundred and fifty thousand dollars. The lady who is taking his job, the new manager for the bank branch, smiles across the desk at him. "You made a decent amount of money over the cost you paid," she notes.

"I suppose so." In the short time she has known Henry, she's known him to look this tired and run down. Rumor has it he was never like this before. He was always full of life and fun. He was interesting and good at his job. The tellers say this change in Henry all started when his wife disappeared almost two years ago.

"Well, you know how all this works, I'm sure. The mortgage loan has been paid in full; here is the receipt for that." She hands him a printed sheet of paper. "Then the extra money has been added to the bank account you asked us to put the money in." She hands him another sheet of paper showing the balance of this account. "You should be all set." She stands, offering him her slim hand. "We all wish you the best of luck, Mr. King."

"Thank you." Henry takes the two pieces of paper, folds

them into squares, and slides them into the back pocket of his jeans. Then he heads out of the bank he has worked in for over a decade and into the car he has owned just as long. Today is the last time he will see either of them. Just like this morning was the last time he would lay eyes on the house where he spent most of his married years. The same house where his wife was last seen. The same house where her blood was found. The house that has been featured on the news, on a special episode of Unsolved Mysteries, and on America's Most Wanted. The house he can no longer face.

Henry drives through the gorgeous tree-lined streets, enjoying every minute of this scenery before it is no longer part of his daily routine. The tall trees with their thick green leaves are not something he will see again soon. The curves in the road and the changes in altitude are also something he will get less of. He rolls down the window and allows the cool air, still with the hint of ocean humidity, to fill the car. If today is about remembering and appreciating what this life had to offer, he will do the best he can to surround himself with all of it.

He drives straight to the airport and parks in the same economy lot where the police found the car owned by Mr. Houston almost two years ago. Conspiracy theorists will tell you they believe that car was used to bring Regina out of the house. They believe her body was thrown into the quarry. Then they believe the car transported Stewart to the airport, where he fled the country. According to the specials which Henry didn't watch but were summarized for him by countless people who did, police believe Stewart also staged the suicides of his own sister and a child pornographer. He was in possession of photographs taken at both of those crime scenes that could only have been taken by someone who was a witness to or an accomplice for both events. If he ever does decide to step foot back in the country, he would be questioned and possibly even arrested for those crimes.

Of course, Henry knows Stewart will not be stepping foot back in the country, but he doesn't talk about that.

A man in an orange vest approaches Henry, who steps out of the vehicle. "Are you Henry?" he asks.

"That's me."

"This the car?"

"Yup." Henry hands the single key to the man. "This is the one."

The man hands him an envelope. "Here's the $500. Thanks for your donation. Have a nice day."

Henry takes the single suitcase containing everything he hasn't sold out of the back seat of the car and heads into the airport. He never even turns around to watch the man load the car up onto the tow truck to bring it down to its new location. He has already said his goodbyes to that part of his former life.

He gets through security with no issues and takes himself to a little restaurant in the correct terminal. He drops onto a barstool, settling his small bag at his feet. "What can I get you?" the bartender asks.

"I'll have a scotch on the rocks. What do you have to snack on?"

"Pretzels, french fries, mozzarella sticks—"

"Fries are great," Henry interrupts. "I'll take those."

"You have a brand of scotch you'd prefer?"

Henry glances over the bartender's shoulder to the wall of glass bottles. Up on the top shelf, his eyes spy a brand label he recognizes with an age he has never tried. "Is that Glenlivet aged eighteen years?" he asks.

The bartender smiles. "It sure is." He leans down toward Henry. "If money is not an issue, I even have a twenty-five year back here."

Henry slides a hundred-dollar bill from the envelope and drops it on the polished wood. "I'll try that twenty-five."

The bartender straightens, his smile widening. "Let me get those going for you right now." He takes the cash and spins to face the register. He clicks a few buttons, and the drawer spits open. He reaches down, counting out some change with his back to Henry.

Then he reaches below the cuff of his shirt, freeing a small key on a single leather strap. Henry watches him use this key to open a locked and lighted cabinet facing the other side of the little restaurant and bar. He pulls out a bottle with a familiar label and pours a hearty dose of the amber liquid into a glass. He brings the drink and a small pile of cash and drops them in front of Henry.

Henry doesn't count the cash, just leaves it sitting there on the bar. He figures it's probably around $40. That isn't a lot to him right now, not with the kind of money he's sitting on from selling everything he owned. For the first time in his life, he's aware that this bartender could use that cash more than he ever could, no matter what this guy's situation is.

His fries arrive when he's only had a small taste of the scotch. It is, without a doubt, the best alcohol he has ever tasted. It makes sense, he supposes; he was only eight years old when this began aging. He was barely in third grade, entirely too young to be aware that there were people in this world who made their living off being paid to end the lives of others.

He munches on his fries, sips his scotch, and lets himself think about the subject he doesn't ever talk about. Regina. He can still remember the first moment he laid eyes on her. They were both working part-time at a retail store. He was working in hardware; she was in women's clothing. He saw her pop out of the fitting room, her arms full of clothing and her hair slipping out of her ponytail to ring around her face. Despite the fact that she should have looked stressed, that anyone else in that position at that time would have looked stressed, he remembers the smile on her face more than anything else. He remembers thinking she'll do well in retail. Customers will like her.

He got up the courage to speak to her in the breakroom that very afternoon. He told her she seemed pleasant, customers would want to buy things from her. He talked her into trying something that earned commission. Her options at that store were limited: washer and dryer combos, car stereo equipment, jewelry, or top-of-the-line sporting goods like treadmills. Only one of those had a department adjacent to his. As luck would have it, that is the one she chose.

For the next year, they worked near each other. He sold hand tools to people, and she sweetly talked them into treadmills. He finished his degree in business; she finished her degree in cybersecurity. He never thought to wonder if the sale of treadmills was her only source of income. Until two years ago, he never wondered if Regina was killing people on the side. Who has to worry about things like that?

Henry checks his watch. He takes the last swig of his drink and motions for the bartender. "Do you know if I can take the rest of these on the flight?" he asks, pointing to the fries.

"Let me get you a little box." He hands him a black carton, one that looks like it should contain Chinese food. "Pop them in here, and no one will give you any trouble."

Henry takes his time dropping them into the box. Then he stands up and collects his bag. The bartender tips his chin toward the bar and the stack of cash still sitting there. "You left your change," he says. His voice is tinged with the excitement of thinking that may be his tip, but he doesn't want to assume. Henry likes him for that.

"It's all yours. Thanks for the service."

He boards the plane last and doesn't mind doing it. He didn't spring for first-class seats. In fact, he hasn't openly spent that kind of money in years in case anyone was watching him. He should hate Regina for putting him through all of this. He knows that. He should hate her for setting him on this road where he had no choice but to cut his losses and start over.

But he doesn't hate her. Not even a little.

That first month after she disappeared, he thought he did. He tried not to think of her at night when he slipped under the covers and felt the cold sheets just beyond his reach. He tried not to think of her when he decided to take her car, and the interior still smelled like her perfume. When he found the note on the computer with bank information, the hatred started to slip just a little. Here was the proof that she loved him too. She prepared to take care of him, even knowing what would happen to her.

Once he started thinking like that, things changed. He noticed she had set the coffee he liked onto a monthly delivery service only a month before she had disappeared and set it to continue for a year before emailing him a request to continue.

Making sure he had coffee, even when she wasn't around to supply it. When the light on the thermostat lit up, telling him it was time to change the air filter, he found a note taped to the closet door with the name of the brand they buy and the size of the filter.

Then, about six months after Regina disappeared, he found the box of carefully written out recipe cards. They were all there. The recipes Henry loved and asked her to make. The ones she claimed were simple and required no recipe. All written out in easy-to-follow steps. He knew she'd done it for him.

He made every recipe in that box. He'd stop at the store on his way home, card in hand, and buy everything he needed. Then he would go home and cook it, following her careful instructions. He'd eat as much as he could. Then he would box up the rest of the food and drop it in the breakroom at work with a note that simply read "help yourself." He did this every night until the recipe box was empty. Then he dropped all the cards back in the box and started again.

By the third rotation, he could make them all without looking at the card.

By the third rotation, he realized the longing for Regina was stronger. He missed everything good about his wife.

It wasn't until a year and a half after her disappearance that he realized he missed the good in her enough to forgive the bad. Right around Valentine's Day, when the tellers were decorating the bank with the red and pink hearts strung all over the place, he realized if Regina was standing in front of him, he would be capable of forgiving her for everything she'd hidden from him. For everything she'd done.

That was when he'd spoken to the corporate office about

leaving. That was when he started the process of selling the house, buying the plane tickets, and putting this in motion. It was time to step away from that life. That life was gone.

Henry has to change planes twice. The sun, moving in the opposite direction from his plane, sets twice and rises once during his flight. By the time he lands for the final time at the International Airport he was destined for, he has barely slept. He should be exhausted. Yet he finds his stomach clenching with anticipation like a child on Christmas Eve, knowing something good is coming.

The first thing he does after getting off the plane is to stop and appreciate the full glass windows and the large lobby. He looks beyond the lobby to the bustling city. It moves like any other city, full of people and cars. But something about it promises new beginnings.

He pops into the exchange, conveniently located in the airport lobby, and swaps all of the cash he is carrying for the local currency. Then he steps onto a bus bound for his next destination, one whose address was difficult to come by. He hopes the information is correct.

At the bus stop, he walks, following the directions he has memorized, to the small apartment units with their backs facing the ocean. He walks up the two flights of stairs and down the hallway until he is standing in front of the unit with the small gold numbers reading "12".

Exhausted from travel and weary of starting this entirely new life, Henry King knocks on the door.

Chapter 32

I SUPPOSE I should start by explaining myself. There is, after all, a little truth missing from the story you've been told. Where shall I start? Don't say the beginning; you've been in the story from the beginning. It's much of the end that you're missing. I suppose I'll start with the day I went missing.

Henry woke up to his 6:30 alarm clock and followed his morning routine. The only difference is that he paused at the entrance to the living room and looked at me for a long time, as if trying to memorize my face. "Goodbye, Regina," he said.

I couldn't find my tongue at that moment. I remember it because I was so tragically incapable of any words that would give meaning to the situation. In the end, I said nothing, and Henry simply left for work. It's one of my biggest regrets, actually. Not being able to find the words to say goodbye to that life. The woman he thought I was—would that woman be capable of giving voice to just the right words? I guess we'll never know.

After he left, I got dressed in simple jeans and an unremarkable t-shirt. I walked down to the bus stop on the corner and boarded a city bus. I rode it down to the rental place in town where Henry had called the night before to make a reservation for a vehicle under the alias Henry Stewart. It seemed fitting and a little funny. I paid cash and drove myself home. There were slight differences between this luxury SUV and the one driven by Stewart Houston, but the tires were exactly the same, and the weight of the two vehicles was close enough. That is all we really needed.

At our house, I backed up to the fence that leads to the backyard. Then I immediately pulled back out and returned to the rental car place. I handed her the keys with a smile. I had been gone for less than an hour. I never even had to put gas in the rental car. All I needed this vehicle for was the tire treads; it had served its purpose.

I took the bus back home and packed a small bag full of things I thought I couldn't live without, including over a hundred thousand dollars in cash. I carefully copied Stewart's handwriting from the note he had slipped in the cash he gave to Henry. I left it propped up on the keyboard where Henry could produce it when he was ready.

I set the bag by the back gate with a roll of gauze, fresh gloves, a plastic bag, and different clothing. Then I headed back to the kitchen where I'd lived peacefully with my husband for most of my adult life for the real show. I had originally wanted to avoid bloodshed. Henry convinced me there was no other way to do it. I'm no stranger to blood, obviously. I had done some research while we were discussing this plan. I had a few ideas where I could draw blood from my own body without doing too much damage. I ran my fingers along the blade of the knives in the block. In the end, I went with my favorite knife for cooking. The basic chef knife.

I ran the blade along my forearm, making a deep cut that

was about five inches long. This is a great place to draw large amounts of blood from a body without actually killing the person. Great for torture or for creating a scene. The pain forced me to close my eyes and take a few ragged breaths. I didn't try to stop the blood, just let it drip onto the floor. Then I ran my knees through it, dragging lines of my own blood across the tile. Henry assured me he would hire professionals to clean it all up.

I left the back door open when I pushed my way out to the backyard. I tossed the knife into the backyard grass, knowing it would be found later. I changed my clothing, stuffing the dirty ones into the plastic bag. I wrapped my arm in gauze and donned the fresh gloves. Then I sealed the plastic bag and took both the plastic bag and the packed bag with me. I left the gate hanging open and walked myself out of the neighborhood. It was the last time I ever saw the cute little street.

I still had my last burner phone tucked into the bag I'd packed. I stopped at a restaurant to grab myself some food and pulled the phone out. While the clerk fulfilled my order, I dialed the number I had recently memorized.

"Innovative IT Solutions," the voice answered.

"Stewart Houston, please."

"May I ask who's calling?" I think I remembered this as the young lady who had met me at the elevator the one time I visited my client at work.

"He's expecting my call. We had a deadline to discuss." The teenager behind the counter brought a bag and nodded in my direction. I winked at him in silent acknowledgment of the fact that we both know it's my food. I appreciated him not calling out the order and ruining my phone call.

I took the bag and headed back out of the restaurant. It

was at this point there was a noise from the other end of the phone. "Hello?" Stewart's voice was confused, questioning.

"Hello, Mr. Houston. I thought I'd call you to tell you about a little change of plans today."

"Regina?" No longer calm, Stewart's voice grew agitated. If he could have reached through the phone at that moment, I would have been concerned about his hands wrapping around my neck.

I sat on the bench at a local bus stop and opened the bag, taking out my chicken sandwich. I knew if the bus was on time, I would have ten minutes. "I'm so glad you recognized my voice," I answered. "Listen carefully. I am going to be at a place called the Shadowbrook Condominiums in about an hour. You're going to meet me there. We're going to chat."

"Why would I ever meet with you?" he practically growled into the phone. The sound of his anger was music to my ears.

"Because, Stewart, I have the money you sent to Henry and something you'll definitely want to take back. See you soon, Mr. Houston." I hung up the phone and ate my sandwich. Then I boarded the bus. My fingers itched to borrow a laptop from someone and check to be sure Stewart hadn't noticed the cameras at his home had been disabled three days ago. But I knew any technology trail was out of the question, not to mention someone might remember the girl who borrowed their laptop. So I rode in silence straight to the bus stop outside of Stewart's house. I jumped over the fence only when I was relatively certain no one was looking. I slipped in the back door, happy when the alarm didn't immediately alert.

It turns out Innovative IT Solutions may have a few holes

in their network that could benefit from my legitimate services. Holes that allow someone nefarious to access personal files housed on the network. Like files with access codes for Stewart's alarms cameras. It was a risk, honestly. If Stewart was the kind of guy who noticed when his devices were offline, he could've simply turned them back on. If he was the kind of guy who lazily relied on the device to notify him if something was amiss, I was safe. I'd never been happier for a lazy client before.

Inside the house, I dropped the box containing a few photographs I'd printed from my personal stash into Stewart's closet and retraced my steps right back out to the bus stop.

The next bus I boarded took me close to the meeting location, where I sat on the ground under a tree to wait. Stewart did not disappoint. He arrived, practically spitting with anger, and stepped out of his running vehicle to confront me. I stood up, waved delicately at him, and wiped off my jeans. "What is the meaning of this?" he called. "What do you have for me?"

I held up a single finger. "Almost."

"Regina, what the hell?" he shouted. "We had a deal. Henry has the money and today is the day. Why are we here?"

"You're going to be my witness. I knew you wouldn't want to miss this or leave anything to chance. You're going to drive me to a location. You're going to walk me to the quarries. You're going to make sure I jump right in. You're going to watch me finish this hit."

His anger deflated in that moment. I remember watching it leave his body on a sigh. "Are you serious? No games?"

"No games." I confidently walked to his car, opened the passenger door, and got in.

Stewart got back in his car and slammed the door.

"Direct me," he commanded.

So I did. I directed him to the spot I wanted him to park, where he was likely to be seen. I told him to park the car, and I led him to the quarries. I stood on the edge of the quarries, looking down to where so many people before me had fallen to their deaths.

Then, it was as simple as you'd imagine.

Stewart was so predictable. He rushed me, perhaps sensing that I would never have had it in me to actually jump. In the end, I read his body language and knelt down at the last moment. I was able to sweep my leg out, taking him out at the calves. Stewart stumbled his way right over the edge of the quarry. It was not a pretty jump by any stretch of the imagination. I watched him hit his head on the way down. I assumed they would find his body, but who knows if that's how it happened.

The rest, as they say, is history. I took the car to the airport myself. I wiped down the steering wheel. I paid cash for a plane ticket and boarded a plane out of the country using my Regina Kingston ID card.

There you have it. The story of how I brought an end to my Stewart Houston problem and my own perfect life with Henry.

Chapter 33

—◆—

THERE IS NO television in the unit I've rented, despite the fact that I rented it furnished. That's one thing Americans will notice when they travel to other places. There are simply some countries in the world where our obsession with television hasn't reached. This happens to be one of them. It also happens to be a small country where extradition to the United States is not practiced. It seemed like good planning to choose a country where that was a rule. I suppose I could make a change now, but it doesn't seem worth it. I like it here. I like my apartment with an entire wall full of paperback books to choose from. I don't miss the mindless hum of the television at all.

The corded phone on the little table beside the couch rings. I put my current read over my thigh and reach for it. "Hello?"

"Rachel?"

"Yes. Who's calling?"

"It's Sandra from the bookstore. Can you possibly come in tomorrow? I know it's your day off, but my kid has a soccer game, and I really want to be able to go. I was just hoping–"

I cut her off. "Totally. No problem."

"Oh my God, are you sure?" she asks, her voice automatically sounding relieved.

"Of course. No problem at all. What time is your shift?"

"Eleven to six."

"I'll be there," I tell her. "Don't stress about it. Good luck at the game."

"Thanks, Rachel. You're the best."

"I know. Bye, Sandra." I hang up the phone and pick up the book again. I read two or three sentences, and then my attention is pulled away from the words to the large windows of the apartment. My unit is on the second of three floors and is just high enough to fully enjoy the view of the ocean. During the summer months, the temperature here is a consistent warm that I still haven't gotten tired of. Every day is sunny and clear. Every day is a beach day. Today is no exception. I let my mind wander as I stare at the beautiful sunlight bouncing off the waves.

This life is practically perfect. I have enough cash to never want for anything again. I took a part-time job at a little bookstore just to give me something to do. I don't need the money. I've made a few friends there. People who are pleasant and easy to talk to. I don't see them outside of work, but they keep trying to get me to open up. Maybe one day I will.

I spend my days reading books, soaking on the beach, or sitting on the patio of my apartment. I'm learning to surf with a small group and a capable instructor. I have no credit cards, an ID in the name of Rachel Kingston, and no services that would put me "on the grid." In fact, even my landlord lets me pay cash for the unit and keeps his own name on the records. He doesn't ask too many questions, which I appreciate.

So, if I have everything I ever wanted, why do I feel so empty?

A knock at the door startles me out of my reverie. I put the book down on the coffee table, not bothering to keep my page, and stand up. My bare feet slap the wooden floor as I cross the unit. "I'm coming," I yell to whoever may be on the other side. It's not the day my rent is due, I didn't order food, and I'm not expecting company. I slow down in the kitchen, which is between the living room and the front door. I reach for the handle of the chef knife in the block on the counter, my fingers caressing the titanium and tingling with excitement. "Who is it?" I call.

There is no answer from the other side of the door.

I pull the knife from the block, and the thrum of anticipation builds. I haven't wielded a weapon like this in a long time. It's like riding a bike; my body turns it for the best angle to inflict pain automatically. I stand in front of the door, my legs braced in a stance that will allow me to be anchored safely for the blow I may have to deliver. Then I unlock the door and open it.

The shock is so absolute that I almost drop the knife.

"Hello, Regina," Henry says. "Can I come in?"

Chapter 34

I CAN'T FIND words for my shock and surprise. Part of me always expected to be found. Maybe a relative of Stewart, since he's not able to find me himself. Maybe a detective who couldn't accept the stories I've told. Only in my wildest fantasies did I let myself pretend it would be my Henry who would track me down and show up at my door.

I step out of the way and let him into the apartment. He puts down a single bag while I close and lock the door behind him.

"Nice place," he says, looking around. "I like the windows." He turns in a full circle, stopping when he is facing me. His face softens, and he smiles. A real Henry smile. "I like the dark hair," he says. "More than I thought I would. Of course, I might have just missed your face so much that I wouldn't care if you had no hair at all." He shuffles, sort of awkwardly. "God, Regina, I miss you so much."

"Henry." It comes out of my mouth like a prayer, quiet and intimate. My eyes fill with tears. Henry is really standing here, in my apartment, complimenting my hair. It's unbelievable. I must be dreaming. Henry, who came up with the plan that wrote me right out of his life. Henry, who told me it was fine to have a little bloodshed in our house if it made it believable. Henry, who knows what I spent my life doing and has never really come to terms with that.

"What are you doing here?" I ask quietly.

"I left it all." He looks over his shoulder toward the couch. "Can we sit?"

I shake myself awake and gesture to it. "Right, of course. Yes, sit. Do you want a glass of water or something?"

"Do you have something stronger?" he asks. "Wine or something?"

Wine. With Henry. My heartbeat speeds up, a sudden deep longing for something so normal practically rendering me incapable of movement. I force myself to nod. "Yeah, of course." I drop the knife back into the knife block and wrap my hand around the cool green glass of the nearest bottle. I watch out of the corner of my eye as he takes a seat on the couch, bouncing a little as if he is testing it out. I pop the cork. Henry picks up the book on the coffee table and flips to the back. I pour the liquid into two wine glasses and leave the bottle on the counter.

"I don't ever remember you going for this type of book before," Henry says. "In fact, that's one of the things I noticed after you left." He takes his wine glass from me and drops the book back on the table, face up. "Everything you told me about yourself and what you did but no books about killers or crime." He tips his head toward the book. "Nothing like that book."

I look down at the cover as if seeing it for the first time, although I've been trying to finish it for three days. The two faces staring straight out at the reader, with the masked figure between them. The cover is red based as if implying blood connects these three figures. A lone female, the potential victim. A strong alpha male, the detective. A masked anonymous figure, the bad guy.

I roll my eyes at it. "Call it therapy," I say, turning my attention back to Henry. "I read it and find the flaws in the writing. There are things that would never work, things that are totally unrealistic. But I'm trying to expose myself to that horror without..." I let my voice trail off.

"So you haven't been..." He swirls his wine, likely looking for the right word. "*Practicing* since you got here?"

I shake my head. Then I'm gripped by a sense of anger. I plop down on the couch opposite him, hard enough to jostle the wine in both of our glasses. "Why are you here?" The anger awakens something inside me that I've let sleep for so long. I let her out. Regina King.

I haven't been Regina King since I boarded that plane so long ago. I feel the slow smile creep over my face. I sit up straighter. "Are you wearing a wire? Did you come here to prove you could find me, Henry? What is this all about?" Even to my own ears, my voice sounds like honey. I am in charge again.

I take a sip of my wine, never taking my eyes off the man I loved for so many years. The only man I ever truly loved. The man I still love, probably will always love.

He mirrors my movements, taking a sip of his wine. Then he sets the glass down on the table and leans on his knees, bringing his face closer to me. "No one else knows where I am. I sold everything and left. I had something important to tell you." He reaches for my hands, but slowly in case I pull away.

I don't. Something in his eyes pulls at a part of me that I

thought I let go of. The part of me that dreams about this man at night when I'm alone. The part of me that knows the reason I haven't been truly happy, the one thing missing from my otherwise perfect life, is this man. He touches my hand lightly at first. Then, when I don't pull away, he slides his fingers until they are underneath mine. Almost of their own accord, my fingers close until we are holding hands.

"I forgive you," Henry says. "That's what I wanted to tell you. I know how hard you worked to set things up for me to be able to keep my life together when you left. I saw it, and I realized I didn't want to do this life without you. Even if it meant that I also had to let it all go and chase you. Even if it meant that I had to come to terms with what you were doing for a living, what you needed to do. I'd rather be in that life, with you, than in the life you left me in alone. Does that make sense?"

Tears slide down my face, and I nod. It makes perfect sense.

He lets go of my hand and touches my thigh, bare under my shorts. The touch awakens some deep yearning inside of me. It must do the same for Henry because his touch gets stronger, more insistent. When he starts to lean toward me, I lean back. So that when he is close enough to finally connect our lips, I'm lying on the couch with him hovering over me. The kiss is deeper and more intense than I remembered. There is a carnal need there, from both of us.

"It's been two years," Henry groans. "Have you been with anyone else?"

"No." My voice comes out breathy, needy. "Have you?"

"No."

He kisses me again, this time tugging at our clothing

with his hands.

Chapter 35

WE LIE NAKED on the couch, our legs entwined and our heads facing the ocean view, catching our breath. My head rests on his chest, letting me feel the heartbeat that tells me all of this is real as opposed to an amazing dream. "How did you find me?" I ask.

Henry sighs. "The bank accounts you left me were the clue, although I didn't see it at first." I can feel the rumble of his words in his chest as he speaks. "I noticed much later that the paperwork for one of the international ones had two names on the account. Regina King and Rachel Kingston. I had already closed the account, but I wondered about it. Eventually, I found this voice modulator app, and I used it to make my voice sound more feminine. I called the bank, said I was Rachel Kingston. Told them I wanted to access my open account. I was taking a gamble that you'd have one. I thought, maybe, the additional name was a clue for me to follow. The lady who answered the phone told me she could access that for me, no problem. Said she just needed a little information. They asked for the date of birth; I gave them yours. They asked for a mother's maiden name; I gave them yours. I figured people share birthdays all the time, Wilson is a popular name, and you would bank on no one having that alias anyway. It worked."

Henry sits up a little, and I slide away from his chest. He looks excited, proud. He likes telling me this story, showing me that he followed the breadcrumbs I left for him. It makes me smile to see him so intense. "So then the hard part came. She asked me for the passphrase. I tried that one quote you always liked: 'in spite of everything, I do believe people are really good at heart,' but that wasn't it. She said something like, 'sorry, honey, that's not the one. Would you like to try again?' So I had to think fast. What would you have set as your passphrase?"

I wonder if he was sitting in the bedroom near the computer desk, where he would've likely kept the bank information when he made this call. Or was he sitting in the living room near the throw pillow that I ordered about a week before my little disappearance routine? The one embroidered especially for this little miracle.

"Then I remembered the pillow that showed up after you left. I told her the phrase was 'absence makes the heart grow fonder.' She let me into the account. Now, she thinks I'm you, so she asks what she can help me with. I tell her I can't remember if I gave the bank my new address. I ask her to tell me what address she has for me. She rambles off an address, this address. I thank her, tell her that is the right one, and then tell her to have a nice day." His grin goes a little lopsided when he smiles down at me. "She told me to tell Hank she said hello."

"Oh," I laugh a little. "Right, I have a habit of telling personal stories to the tellers at the banks whenever I use my new name. It helps them to remember me. I want them to remember Rachel and this whole life of Rachel's. Anything that helps ensure they have this whole persona, you know?"

Henry pulls himself free of me a little, leaning toward the back of the couch. Then he launches himself over me, reaching for something. I laugh. "What are you doing?"

He sits up, now holding the jeans he had discarded on the floor earlier. He pulls a wallet out of the back pocket. "Showing you something." He slides an ID card out of the wallet and hands it to me. "I got this after that phone call. This is what I used to buy the plane ticket—in cash, of course. It's also what I've used since I got here."

It's a traveler's ID card, the same kind I have. It shows that the cardholder is an American citizen authorized for world travel. It makes getting other documents in other countries easier. They are expensive forgeries, but they are worth every penny. This one has Henry's picture and date of birth. But the name, Hank Kingston, is all new.

I cock my head to the side and look at him. "Hank?"

"It was your idea. I just followed the trail you left." He takes the ID and slides it back into the wallet. He drops the wallet and the jeans on the floor. "You wanted me to find the name Rachel. You wanted me to find the account. You wanted me to find the address. You wanted me to find Hank. There's no one else who knows those accounts ever existed, no one else you left all this for. You wanted me to find you, didn't you?"

I nod, feeling a little blush creep into my cheeks. "I hoped you would try someday. It was so risky...but I had to give you something, just in case."

"I'm here now. It's all going to be fine." He wraps me in his arms and snuggles in close. I want to believe him, but there's still this looming thing between us. I need him to realize that the part of me that he loathes is not going away.

I push away from him and stand up. "You didn't do anything to wipe Henry out, right? He's just gone. You could still go back?"

He sits up. "Why would I do that?"

"What if I told you I killed someone else? What if I told you that's how I'm living here so cheap? I killed the landlord and dumped his body out in the ocean."

To his credit, he doesn't look shocked or disgusted. He scrunches up his eyes like he's thinking, screwing his lips into an almost frown. "Where did you get a boat?"

"What?" I shake my head. "Irrelevant question. I could rent one. Say I killed someone. You could live with that?"

He clicks his tongue like he's finding the rhythm for whatever he is about to say. "Yes, I could live with that. I'd have a lot of questions—did he deserve it, are you sure you weren't caught, are we safe here? But I could live with it."

His expression is completely neutral, calm. I stand there, shocked, looking into the face of complete honesty. I drop back onto the couch. "I didn't kill my landlord; that wouldn't even be my style. He's a decent guy, and he charges me a fair rent. I haven't actually killed anyone since Stewart."

Henry taps the paperback on the coffee table. "But you think about it."

I nod. "I think about it a lot."

Henry stands up. "Alright, enough about work. I'm starving, and that ocean is calling my name. Let's get dressed and then you can take me somewhere to get some food. We'll practice this whole Rachel and Hank routine. I think Rachel and Hank like red wine and putting their bare feet in the ocean.

What do you think?"

I smile at my husband. The energy he is exuding right now is the exact opposite of the me I have been for two years. I'm stay in and curl up with a book; he's dance in the street and walk in the ocean. He is what has been missing in my life for two years. I stand up. "Let's do it."

Chapter 36

I TAKE HENRY to my favorite local restaurant. Although the employees here speak the native tongue, most of them also speak English. They wave at me when I step into the back of the restaurant. "Nasi Katok?" he calls, referring to my favorite dish. I hold up two fingers, and he nods.

"What's Nasi Katok?" Henry asks.

"Rice, chicken, and a sauce called sambal. Great flavor. You'll love it." I point to the left-hand side of the restaurant toward an open door that leads to an outdoor patio near the ocean. "We can sit out there. He'll bring it to us."

"You come here often," Henry notes, not really a question.

"A few times a week. I really like the atmosphere." We step out onto the patio, and the smell of the ocean makes me smile. Henry chooses a small, round wooden table and drops onto the bench.

The cook who recognized me comes out of the door holding two small white plates. "Missus Rachel, you want coffee or coconut milk today?" He sets the plates before us. "Who your friend?"

"I'm Hank, and coconut milk for me."

"Same," I say. "Hank is new to the country. Any advice for him?"

The man pinches his lips and narrows his eyes. "You new here, you get job and help out. We all work together. We pitch in."

Henry nods. "I'm not afraid of hard work. Do you need some help here part-time? Maybe picking up the tables or something?"

"You know how to use broom and mop?" he asks, looking Henry up and down.

"I sure do."

He nods. "You start tomorrow. Ask for me." He lays his hand on his chest. "Jin."

Henry offers his hand. "Nice to meet you, Jin." The two men shake hands before Jin disappears back into the building.

"Look at that. My first day here, and I already have a job," Henry says.

Jin comes back and sets down two glasses of coconut milk. Then we're alone again. It's quiet enough while we eat that we can hear the sound of the waves slapping the shore below us. Henry turns in his chair, watching the ocean for a bit. "I see why you like this place," he says. "The ocean is calming."

"It's pretty much always this warm, too," I tell him. "You'll really love it here." I let the silence regain its footing as we finish our plates. Then I push mine away from me toward the center of the table and lay my palms in front of me. "Alright, enough stalling. Tell me what the news reported. Tell me what happened back home. I didn't follow the story at all."

Henry takes a deep breath in through his nose and blows

it out. "They declared Regina"—he raises his eyebrows questioningly in my direction—"dead about a year after she disappeared. They found the car at the airport and assumed Stewart fled. After an investigation at his house turned up some photographs only a witness to a few suicides would have, they concluded he must have fled the country to avoid being caught up in anything. According to the most recent information search, they are searching for him as a person of interest in all three cases."

"Any changes to the ruling on the suicides?"

"Not that I'm aware of."

I take a moment to process what all of this means. When I left, there was always the fear that something would go wrong. I worried they would accuse Henry, maybe find out about the rental car that we used Rachel Kingston's ID for and paid cash to rent. The one that was the same size and weight as Stewart's. The one with the same tires. I worried they'd find Stewart's body, although I was pretty sure there was nothing on his person to tie him to me. I worried the pictures alone wouldn't be enough to throw suspicion onto Stewart for the other deaths. Or that the cash trail would bring us down. I worried about a lot of things.

Henry being here is still the best surprise, but this is the best news. The news that we truly got away with it. We are free.

Chapter 37

<hr>

HANK HAS BEEN in town a week. I'm sitting on a folding beach chair he bought, which resides directly on the beach under my patio now. The sun is beating down on my face and keeping me warm while I enjoy the sight of him swimming, his perfect breaststroke bringing a smile to my face. I continue to watch him as he comes up out of the ocean swells, hair wet and body glistening. He shakes himself off as he comes closer. Then he drops into his own identical chair beside me. "This is the life," he moans. He throws his hands back behind his head and closes his eyes.

It is. He's right. We both have small part-time jobs that we do just for fun. We spend all our days on the beach, right here. We have amazing sex, we eat great food, and we enjoy each other. That should be the end of the story...and it would be except for this unscratchable itch inside me. That burning need to see more death.

Something inside me has changed. When that girl died in the car accident all those years ago, it was an epiphany for me.

A moment where I realized how much I enjoy death. Stewart's death was another one. Before Stewart, I had only ever killed who I was hired to kill or by accident. Stewart was the first intentional victim of my own choosing. It felt more powerful, more emotional, more exhilarating.

I turn on my side, facing the only person in the world who claims to be able to accept me as I am. "Hank." My voice must sound serious because he opens his eyes and turns to face me. "We have to talk."

"I'm listening."

I look around the beach, making sure no one else is around. As usual, we have the area all to ourselves. "I don't think I can stop. But the way I was doing it before was dangerous. I think I want to go freelance. No cash exchanged, no other people."

He nods as if what I have told him is as easy to understand as if I had said I think I want to buy a new car. Maybe it is right now. Maybe that's what two years apart forced him to analyze.

I watch his face as I drop the next piece of information, waiting to see his reaction. "I also think I found my first victim."

Henry's face gives nothing away. Then he turns on his side and uses his elbow to prop up his head. "Tell me the story, then," he says. "Let's make sure it's believable."

About the Author

Tabatha Shipley is an author, avid reader, and book addict from Arizona. She has an amazing husband, two remarkable children, and one really quirky dog. She can often be found on social media raving about whatever book she is most recently obsessed with. Find her to join in on the obsession and add to her TBR with your favorite titles.

tabathashipleybooks.com